"It takes a master," wrote the Publisher's Weekly in its review of Gordon R. Dickson's most recent massive novel, TIME STORM, *"to handle the concepts involved here..."*

The word Master describes Gordon Dickson. Winner and recipient of the Nebula, the Hugo, the British Fantasy, and the Skylark Awards, he is the creator of the Childe Cycle, a lifework of twelve novels covering a time span of a thousand years, nineteen years to date in the writing and with eight novels yet to be written. *"A proper interpretation of the Childe Cycle is possible only in the light of the recent work of controversial European mythologist Georges Dumezil..."* in the words of critic Sandra Miesel.

From the Childe Cycle come the well-known Dorsai mercenaries, the Exotics philosophers, and the Friendlies, near-superhuman future Splinter Cultures of the present-day human race once it has moved out among the stars. His forty successful books include many other memorable characters, human and alien — Hokas (with Poul Anderson), Dilbians, Space Bats, human colonists and the Outposters who guard them, Star Scouts, hi-lifters, rebels, adventurers, a Prince of a Thousand Worlds ... and more.

It is Gordon Dickson's particular genius that on the large canvases of his books he is able to bring to life real people, believable intelligent animals and aliens, all caught together in the web of future history extrapolated firmly and rigorously from the present. World-wide, over three million copies of his books have been sold; and now, in the seventies, a host of new readers are discovering him.

HOME
FROM
THE
SHORE

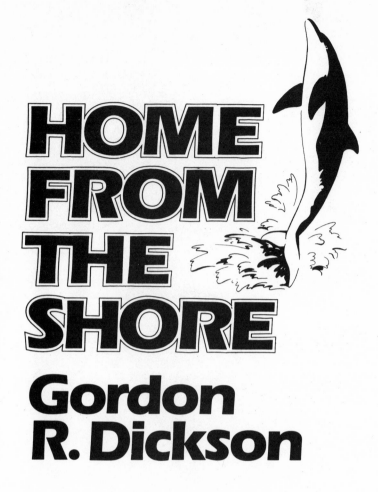

HOME FROM THE SHORE

Gordon R. Dickson

Artwork

James R. Odbert

SUNRIDGE PRESS

A Division of Charter Communications, Inc.
A Grosset & Dunlap Company
Publishers • New York

This book is dedicated to
Tom Doherty,
who by his concern with it
made possible a long-standing dream.

Foreword

What lies between the covers of this book represents an attempt that is unique, not only in science fiction but in publishing. Only the thesis that anything can happen explains it—except that in this case it is the sort of anything that lurks beyond the ordinary dreams of most artists and writers. In fact, in my twenty-seven years as an author previously I had seen nothing to suggest that there might be a practical possibility of arranging the kind of mutual creation that produced this book in its present form.

Nearly a year ago at the time of this writing, Tom Doherty, publisher of Ace Books, spoke to me about an idea of his, not realizing how closely it matched one of my own, which had, in fact, been in mind for a number of years. That long-held idea was a plan for rewriting one of my earlier works to my exact satisfaction and furnishing it with illustrations made to my direction, which would exactly fit the story and interpret it as I had originally wished it interpreted. The plan had laid in the back of my mind all these years, unfulfilled, because I had seen no possibility of putting it into execution, except by publishing such a book at my own expense.

Now, independently, I had been approached with Doherty's idea, which was that one of my early writings be expanded and illustrated with the work of an artist of my choice. Ace Books, he indicated, could bring me and the artist together into New York, where we could discuss the book and the illustrations to be done.

This offer was the first of two happy coincidences. The second, was that just at that time, by good fortune, there was an artist named James Odbert in my home area, whom I considered an ideal choice to do the illustrations for such a book as Doherty had in mind. I made the suggestion, therefore, that instead of our making use of an artist whom I would be able to meet with only once and briefly in New York, Odbert be asked to do the artwork. He and I lived only the width of a city apart; and we would be able to get together as often as the work required.

Moreover, there was another reason which made him the ideal choice as an artist to work with me on the book. Like me, he was deeply interested in the Polynesian culture on which the culture of the sea people in the book was based; and he had made a study of it during a two year stay in Hawaii. Vital to the story of HOME FROM THE SHORE was the special feeling of belonging, the *nous-nous,* of the sea people; which Odbert not only also understood but to which he responded—see the illustration on page 97. In effect, we spoke the same language in this area, and the fact that we did would be critical to a successful making of the book as I envisioned it.

It was settled, therefore; and James Odbert agreed to work with me on HOME FROM THE SHORE. The work itself turned out to be full of discoveries for both of us. The profusely illustrated story that the book presently is, with over fifty pages of Odbert illustrations, developed eventually into something not merely new in bookmaking but in artistic concept. The end result of our teamwork eventually became a collaboration in the truest sense of that word between the artist and the author. What emerged was not merely an illustrated story, not even a story with special illustrations carefully fitted to it; but a unique unit of pictures integrated with words in which these two elements became equal partners.

There were a number of factors involved in this. Primary to the rest was the fact that the work to be done was the product of a collaboration between an artist who was in love with the story and an author who was profoundly impressed with the capabilities of the artist. The effect of this was that Odbert and I each fell almost immediately into the practice of leaning on the other for strengths outside our own creative area, to the great benefit of the work itself. Involved in this, and made necessary by it, was an astonishing amount of conferencing—many times over what I had envisioned when I had first urged that I work with an artist living in close proximity to my own working area. Odbert and I found ourselves continually concerned with matching the fine details of the art to those of the story and those of the story to that of the art. The end result was a situation in which each of us fed off and gained from the creative imagination of the other.

There have been instances in this book, for example, of Odbert making suggestions to me, and my making suggestions to him, that rang almost eerily in accordance

with what the other had himself been thinking. One of the
other of us would, separately and independently, con-
ceive of something to be done with the book, and hasten
to tell it to the other only to discover that the other had
been only waiting a chance to suggest it himself. A very
clear example of this type of parallel thinking are the
pictures of the two sea-sisters on pages 26 and 27. Odbert
drove over to see me specifically to suggest this illustration and found that I had been eager to seem him so as to
suggest it to him.

The resultant creation has consequently become
this something which is more than a book in the tradi-
tional sense. If we have done what we think we have
done, what you hold now is a mechanism for the imagination never developed before—a magic box of sorts that
the reader can open on an experience more fully ren-
dered than those in ordinary books, putting himself or
herself into the life of the story with an extra element of
depth or involvement which comes from the direct interaction between the subtleties of the text and the subtleties
of the illustration. And it is my belief that as such it
marks the first exploration of a hitherto-untouched area
in book making.

Illustrations were always considered a part of books
up until the early part of this century, when they began to
be crowded out from most fiction for reasons of publisher's cost. The only exceptions to this trend were in
fiction written for the young; and even for this sort of
reading matter they were severely curtailed. A book-
maker's misconception grew into general acceptance to
the effect that it was words, and words alone, that adult
readers wanted, not pictures.

As often happens in the literary field, this misconception was generated and accepted without any real

referendum of those most concerned with it—the readers themselves. The result, consequently, was that it existed very nearly until the present historical moment, with one exception. The exception was in science fiction, the one area of literature where the readers had an opportunity to respond directly to the authors both in person, and by letter; and where, accordingly, they had strongly expressed their preference, not only for illustration in the books they read, but for good illustration—illustration not merely expressed in the poster-like colors of the moment's fashion and sideshow patterns of advertising, without any real concern for the story to which it applied. The illustration the readers showed a desire for was that which truly mirrored the story it illustrated; and which tried to bring into sharp, artistic focus the general images of the characters and scenes forming in the mind as the story was read.

It was toward this sort of illustration and its particular effectiveness that our work on HOME FROM THE SHORE has been directed. For it seems certain, now approaching the end of the twentieth century as we are, that the dispersion of the arts has gone far enough, and that in turning back, as James Odbert and I have here, to the paired unity of word and picture, we are merely part of a general return, now commencing, to the basic intent of all craft, which is to reach the reader, the viewer, the listener—the appreciator in all forms—by any and all artistic means at our disposal.

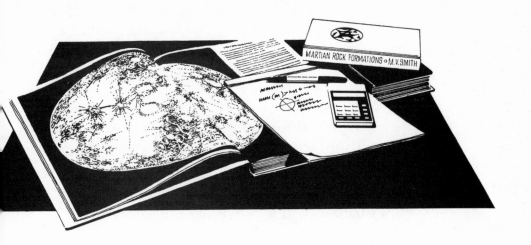

Chapter 1

The night before the sea-born among the senior space cadets were due to ship out—the night before they were to leave Earth to actually witness an attempt at a space bat capture—the chanting of the cadets from the land began early. It was heard down in the quadrangle of the Space Academy, between the two tall barrack buildings, that of the sea-people and the one housing the landers. The sound of massed voices echoed like the growling of penned animals up from the dark shadows of the ground level. It bounced off the walls of the two buildings and entered through the windows of the sea-born cadets, open to the soft New Mexico evening. At his desk, working with his books on the geology of the inner planets, Johnny Joya heard it in his ears and felt it in his bones.

"... *slug a slug a slug a slug!*

"*Slug a sea-slug, slug a slug ...*"

He forced it from his mind. But only a few
minutes later his door opened—without warning,
for among themselves the sea-born did not knock,
knowing as they knew so many things about each
other, when they were welcome and when they were
not. He looked up to see Mikros Palamas, standing
at his elbow.

"They've got to stop that," Mikros said.

Johnny's gaze read the strong, rectangular
face of the other, who was Representative for
those sea-born cadets in their junior year at the
Academy, as Johnny himself was Representative for
the senior sea-born, the first of them all to have
accepted the landers' invitation to enroll. Like
Johnny, Mikros looked big but not alarmingly
so—even, perhaps, a little soft-bodied and harmless
like the sea-slugs for whom the lander cadets
had nicknamed them. But looks were deceiving.

"Don't even think about going down there,"
Johnny said.

"None of us want to go," Mikros said.
"But it hurts us more than they know, that chanting.
We aren't built to take all that hate and fear
they're throwing out. No one is. Our class sent
me up to ask you to call a meeting of the four
class reps."

"A meeting won't do any good," said Johnny.
"And no one's to go down. No one."

"It's hard not to."

"They aren't going to stop just because some of us go ask them to," Johnny said, "and if they saw just a few of us down there they might do something foolish. Seeing us just rubs it in to them, makes it worse for them."

"They won't come in here," said Mikros, bleakly. "If they'd just come in—but they won't try that."

"Of course not," said Johnny.

It was true. There were probably over a thousand lander Space Academy cadets in the darkness below, now, and less than four hundred of the sea-born in their dormitories. But even the landers would not go to the extent of using weapons in a raid on the other building; and without weapons they did not stand a chance against young men and women grown to physical maturity in the endless waters of the oceans.

"All we need to do is ignore them," said Johnny slowly, patiently repeating the familiar words. "Just six months more until we seniors graduate. Then there'll be some of us in space alongside the landers. We'll be their partners. Keep your mind on that, Mikros, and tell your classmates to keep their mind on it. Up here on the top floor we've had a year more of this than even you juniors; and we've ridden it out, the way

you'd ride out a hurricane up on the surface.
So hang on six months more. We'll graduate and then
the land can't say any longer the sea-born're
unfit for space. And the difference between sea
and land can start to heal."

"It'll never heal," said Mikros. "They hate
us because we're bigger and better than they are.
We'll always be bigger and better. How can
anything heal?"

"Put plugs in your ears. Cover your head
with a pillow. They'll be stopping in an hour
or so because they have to study, too. Wait it out,
Mikros, and tell the others to. Because it's got
to heal. If it comes to war, they can kill us all."

"All right," said Mikros wearily. The skin
over the big bones of his face was tight and
his mouth was one straight line. "I'll go back and
tell them once more . . . we wait a while longer."

"Just a few more months," Johnny said.
"I tell you, it's us seniors up here they're
trying to break—not the rest of you. Six months,
and there'll be no point in their chanting out
there. We'll have graduated a class and got
commissions. We'll have won and they'll have
lost—this try of theirs to keep us from space.
Keep telling our people that, Mikros. It's us
seniors they're after; and if we can stand the
chanting, they can too."

Home from the Shore   19

"All right," said Mikros. "Once more."

He went out.

After he had gone Johnny sat alone,
listening to the voices. His own words repeated
themselves in his head. He had been the one who
had most urged and pushed the coming of the
sea-born here to the Academy. He and his cousin
Patrick—Patrick of the magic musical instruments
and magic voice—had been the two most listened-to
among the third generation of those who had first
begun to call themselves the sea people, the
fourth generation of those who had permanently
turned their backs on the land to live completely
in the oceans, underwater and on the continental
shelves, or completely in movement about the seas.

In a real sense it was he, alone, who had
led the best of the third-generation sea-born
into this. The land had wanted them for their
superior physical strength, their saner minds,
those new, or perhaps old, instincts that the
landers themselves did not have. And he—
idealizing the situation in which he now saw
there was nothing to idealize—had thought he had
seen a chance to end the land's growing jealousy
of his own, free people who had all the wide oceans
of the world to live in.

Instead, he had led the others of his
generation to this place; and the landers'

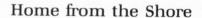

inferiority complex, maturing into
hatred, had, instead of being
reduced, grown now greater than
ever, its increase now echoing
in the voices from the lander cadets
down below.

He went back to his books;
and around eleven o'clock the
chanting in the quadrangle
dwindled and stopped.

The following dawn after
morning parade the sea-cadets
gathered their personal gear
and filed aboard low-altitude
transports lined up on the
Academy airfield. One by one the
boxy-looking flying platforms with
their transparent roofs of light-
sensitive glass took off and
lumbered southeast through
the skies to the shuttle field
at Albuquerque, New Mexico.
There they landed and
the cadets went by
people-mover to the shuttle.

Four hours later, they were in orbit and
leaving the shuttle for the spaceship itself.
None of them had ever been in a space-going
vessel before. They came aboard, however,
with the practised movements that were the
result of many hours of training in the mock-ups
on the ground back at the Academy. A long
double-file of them passed through the main

EARTH—ORBIT
SHUTTLE

airlock into the rear third of the ship, saluting
the duty officer as they came in, then continuing
in a single file down one of the two corridors
that led to assigned quarters on each side of
the aft section.

Johnny found himself near the front of the
file directed down the starboard corridor. To
his right and left as he went along were the
doors of the tiny, personal rooms that would be
home for each of them during the trip. It was
strange to feel the carpet underfoot, to see the
picture-screens inset in the walls, with scenes
that tried to imitate the three-dimensional Earth,
as seen from the window of a lander structure.
There were few scenes of the sea—and none at
all of the undersea.

Like all of his generation among the
sea-born, Johnny listened to his feelings and
perceptions to an extent inconceivable to a
lander. In the sea they had moved away from the
heavy, omnipresent technology of the land.
They were used to and reached out for direct
contact with the living universe of water that
surrounded them—and for all their Academy
training, their instinctive image of space
vehicles had hardly progressed from the romantic
period of their grandparents who had first moved
out into the underseas.

The carpets, the picture screens, the
imitation wood panelling of the metal making up
the walls and doors around him now all seemed
false and almost pitiful in their attempt to carry
the image of a lander earth into space.
Particularly this was so, contrasted to the old
image of bare-metalled, utilitarian craft out
of the dawn of the space age. This, a more
modern ship than the ships of his youthful
dreams, ironically seemed old-fashioned, ornate
and fussy.

"John Joya?" said the Space Force lieutenant
checking them into their rooms. He made a mark
with his light pencil on the coder he carried,
when Johnny nodded. "Right. Twelve-B.
This is yours."

"Thank you, sir." Johnny pushed through the
door indicated and found himself in an apparently
bare closet. But this, too, was as it had been
in the mock-up practises. He reached high on
the wall, opposite the door, pulled down the desk
surface at which he would be studying and working,
and put his personals bag upon it. Then, turning,
he went about the other walls, folding out bed
and chair, opening clothes-locker, bookcases and
stowage compartments.

Satisfied finally that all the room's
appurtenances were clean, available and in working

order, he began to unpack. He was just hanging
the last of his clothing in the locker, the room
set on study mode with the desk still down but
the bed up, and seating surfaces taking up the
space it had occupied, when the door opened
without warning.

It was, of course, one of the sea-born who
came in. A lander would have needed to hear
him answer before knowing entrance was agreeable.
The Cadet Commander of the Senior Class,
Peri Tashkent, stepped in.

"Something wrong, Peri?" Johnny asked, for
her slim, oval face was drawn into serious lines.
Almost as tall as Johnny, she looked at
him soberly.

"Something personal," she said. "That's
why I'd like you to be the one to talk to them
about it. They've given me the number one room on
portside, and Mayal ended up in room sixty-eight,
away back down the line on starboard. It's not
only the distance. That's going to put us in
different watches."

"Of course," said Johnny. Peri and
Mayal Dumayne were sea-sisters.

"It's not as if we can't survive the time
we're out in space with a hello and wave from
time to time," said Peri. "But Ykari Dhu was the
one they put into room two next to me and he's

perfectly willing to trade with Mayal. There
doesn't seem to be any good reason why the duty
officer won't let them. But he won't."

"You'd like me to ask him for you?"

"If you don't mind. Unless you know some
reason why it can't be done."

"I don't," said Johnny. "I'll ask him.
Just a minute while I finish stowing the last
of my things here."

Peri led him down to the end of the corridor
and across to the port side of the spacecraft.
At the last minute, she hesitated.

"You might have better luck if I'm not there,"
she said. "He's geared up to disagree with me."

"Maybe you're right," said Johnny.
"All right, I'll go on alone."

He left her and started down the corridor.

"His name's Shiefer," she called after him.
"He's a lieutenant."

He was, in fact, the same lieutenant who had
checked Johnny into his room, a trim man in his
late thirties with thinning brown hair and
sharp blue eyes.

"Aren't you from over on starboard?" he asked
as Johnny came up. He glanced at his coder.

"That's right, sir. I've already got my
room," Johnny said. "But I'm also representative
for the sea-born Senior Class."

The blue eyes sharpened.

"Something wrong, Mr . . ."

"Joya. Johnny Joya, sir."

"Something wrong, Cadet Joya?"

"Just a minor problem." Johnny spoke slowly and casually as he had learned to speak to the lander cadre at the Academy. "You've got a cadet named Peri Tashkent in room one, here. She spoke to you, I think, about Ykari Dhu—who's in next to her—trading places with another cadet named Mayal Dumayne, over on portside. Is there any particular reason why they can't trade rooms and assignments?"

"If we start it with them, we'll have everybody wanting to trade. This is space, not a picnic outing." The lieutenant almost peered at Johnny. "Why do they have to be in adjoining rooms, anyway?"

"They're sea-sisters," said Johnny. He had sympathized from the start with Peri and her problem of explaining the matter to a lander. Sea-sisters had no counterpart ashore; any more than had sea-friends, the family customs of the People and innumerable other matters that were part of the very fabric of society and existence

to the third generation of the sea-born. Aside
from the difficulty of making the concept of
sea-sisters comprehensible to a lander like this,
there would be a personal element for Peri
herself in making such an explanation. It was
easier for someone outside the relationship
to do it.

"Sisters?" the lieutenant was saying.

"Not blood sisters—sea-sisters," said Johnny.
"It's a matter of choice, starting at a very
early age. They grow up together and they're
very close."

It was a weak explanation of the essentially
psychic kinship that could spring up between
two sea-born of the same age. There was a
sensitivity and awareness to that relationship
that the land could not know, matching the two
individuals to the point where they could almost
read each other's minds. Only the unusual
strength of individual wills in Patrick and
himself had prevented sea-brotherhood between
him and Johnny.

"Close?" The lieutenant was frowning.
"What do you mean—*close?*"

"I mean they're very much alike," said Johnny,
still trying to give the other something he could
understand in lander terms. "So alike that
they're almost one person. Like natural,

identical twins. Only, as I say, in this case
there's no family relationship between them."

The lieutenant shook his head slightly.

"No," he said. "No. That's not enough of
a reason to go making changes. As I said, if
I let them switch everyone's going to want to."

"They won't, sir."

"Oh? Why?" the lieutenant gave him a hard
grin. "What makes you so sure? Aren't there
more of these sisterhoods among the cadets we've
got on this cruise?"

"Well, yes, there are," said Johnny. "But—"

"But what's so different about—" he
glanced at his coder and tapped buttons with
one finger, "Cadet Tashkent and her friend, that
makes them unique?"

Johnny played his last card.

"Cadet Tashkent is Cadet Commander for the
Senior Class."

"Oh?" the lieutenant's face changed. He
looked startled and a little wondering, then
almost suspicious. "She didn't tell me that."

"It wouldn't have occurred to her to, sir."

"Well, of course . . ." the lieutenant tapped
buttons on his coder again. "The Cadet
Commander's entitled to some special consideration.
All right, it's done. But she should have
told me. It does her credit that she didn't want to

use her rank, but it would have saved us all
a lot of trouble."

"Yes sir."

It was the right result for the entirely
wrong reason. Peri and Mayal would have been
insulted by the idea that their special rapport
was so light a thing that it could be made the
tool of a desire to pull Cadet rank.

Johnny saluted and left. Like all the
others, he had been hoping that once they were
into space with actual, working Space Force
personnel, a lot of the misunderstanding between
landers and themselves would evaporate. Instead,
he began to fear that out here, if anything, the
difference between sea and land cultures might
be intensified. Hopefully, he would turn out to
be wrong in this.

He did not. And the difference the sea-born
felt came to localize itself in paneled walls
and the simulated depth-dimensional, antique
landscapes in the artificial windows along the
corridors, in every cabin and wardroom. These
constructs had been meant to alleviate the shock
and loneliness of being away from the familiar
Earth; but one of the extra senses evoked by
ocean living made such devices useless to the
sea-born, who responded only to that which was
real and alive.

"I'll agree the picture-screens work for the
landers, if that's what they claim," Joaquin Loy
said to Johnny on the fifth day out of Earth
parking orbit, when they were alone for a moment,
on duty in the chartroom. "I'll take it on faith,
if that's what they want from us, that all this
imitation of planetside means something to them.
But, Johnny, I really can't believe it, not down in
my guts. Maybe it's true, and they don't feel how
false it is, like we do; and maybe again, they
can't feel the steel walls beyond the screens, and
space, and the stars beyond that. But they have
to *know*, intellectually know, that these pictures
and things are fakes—so how can it be any real
help to them?"

"Because it is," Johnny said. "That's just
one of the differences they have from us, that
is all. They can trick themselves and get some
comfort from it. We can't. That's all."

"Then how are they and we ever going to get
together?" demanded Joaquin.

Johnny shook his head; and a moment later the
cadre officer in charge of the chartroom came back
in, so that there was no more chance for private talk.

Their transport continued to fall, outward
from the sun toward the orbit of Mars; and Johnny
found himself becoming excited over the prospect
of their flight, after all. The sea-born all had

felt a call into space—so like the calling of the
sea to them. Perhaps on this trip he and the other
sea-born would be able to learn things about the
space bats that the landers had never discovered.
Learning anything was difficult, for the bats
reportedly had always died when captured. For
one thing no one understood why the bats were
normally only to be found beyond Mars orbit. It was
true one would occasionally be seen somewhat closer
than that to the sun. But the general assumption
had been that they were planoforming creatures
who sailed the sea of space under the pressure of
light from the various stars and presumably used
light for sustenance. It might be something about

being closer to the sun
than Mars orbit which was
painful or distressful to them.

    Perhaps, thought Johnny, that something might
be something non-physical but nonetheless strong
—like the feeling of unnaturalness that came on
the sea-born themselves whenever they came ashore.
To the space bats, it was theorized, the
apparently empty void was a place of great currents
and pressures—some of them violent, perhaps—as
well as other things imperceptible

to humans. That space was in fact such a place,
the sea-born felt instinctively; and they talked
about that aspect of it as their transport moved
away from the sun.

"It's so full of life out there—"
Albert Paredho, one of the oldest of the seniors,
gestured at the landscaped wall of their wardroom,
beyond which was the hull and the endlessness of
space—"It quivers. I suppose that's one more
thing that the landers don't feel."

"What makes you so sure they don't?" Joaquin
asked. "They could be pretending not to because
they want to see our reactions to it. How
about that, Johnny?"

"I don't know," Johnny had to say, once more.
"But there's no point in our mentioning it to them
until they mention it to us. Is space bothering
you, Joaquin?"

"I'm having some trouble sleeping,"
Joaquin said. "And I've talked to a few others who're
having the same. It's not unpleasant, but . . . you close
your eyes and lie back. It's dark, and these
sorts of jagged, electric lines of light start
sliding back and forth in your head."

"It can't be helped," said Johnny. "We have
to live with it, that's all."

"Then you haven't felt it, yourself?"

"Yes," Johnny said. "I've felt it too."

He had. But for him it had taken on a
different form than that reported by Joaquin. To
him the blackness had seemed one long endless
eternity, one endless depth of living velvet. It
was true that he could feel the web of great
forces running through it. But the velvet itself
was what fascinated in his case. It was a velvet
alive but permeable; so that other living forces
could pass through it, as they and the landers and
the ship were passing through it—as the planets
themselves passed through it with their great cargos
of life of all kinds, from the lowest one-celled
animal and even smaller viruses, to the elephant
and the great blue whale, now extinct. The feelings
peaked in him—the feelings peaked in them all—as
they passed Mars orbit and reached the territory of
space where the great semi-transparent space bats
were to be found.

Two ship's days later, at a hundred and eighty
thousand miles beyond Mars orbit, they picked up
their first bat on the scanning equipment. But its
blip stayed on their screens for only a few seconds,
then disappeared. At a distance, such as this one
had been, the very fact of the bat's turning
sideways to the scanning sweep caused it to drop
out of view. In the next four days they picked up
two more blips, but lost both—one after a five
hour chase.

"We've only got five days out here," said
Joaquin. "We'll never catch up with one in that time."

But on the fourth day they picked up one and
it was not able to lose them. Given a close
discovery of any bat whose relative velocity
was not too high, it was impossible for the
creature to escape. The ship was not only more
maneuverable, but capable of accelerations far
beyond the bat's ability; for under the light-push
these space creatures built velocity slowly, and their
changes of direction were effected only gradually.
Beyond that push they had a very limited ability
of movement, some kind of propulsive system in
which they threw off tiny amounts of bodily mass
at high velocities—the mechanics of which humans
had not yet pinned down.

So the ship closed swiftly with this latest
prey, once the velocities of the two were close
to being matched. Aboard, there was a flurry
of activity.

"Suit up!" roared the amplified voice of the
duty officer over the intercoms.

There were suits—really small one-man space
vehicles—for only a little more than one-third
of the cadets. The rest would have to watch
through monitor screens tied to one or other of
the suits of those lucky enough to leave the ship.

Johnny, in the upper third of his class academically,
was one of those who rated a suit. He had been
through this drill with mockups back on Earth a
thousand times; but now he felt a weird, almost a
lightheaded, feeling as he fitted himself into
the massive, mechanically-appendaged globe.
Once within it, locked in the webbing of his
harness, with the vision screen inches from his
eyes, and his fingers resting on the keys of the
controls, the feeling lessened, but it was still
there as the chamber about him decompressed
explosively, and shot him in his suit into the
airlessness beyond the ship's skin.

He activated the suit's vision screens. Other
personnel were already out of the ship and their
number in the near vicinity of it was increasing
rapidly. The bat was being paced steadily now
by the ship; and the suited men and women who
would try to make the capture shared the same
intrinsic velocity as the ship and the bat.
To Johnny, it was as if they were all at rest in
space, the only indication of motion being the
rippling of the several-miles wide body of the bat,
as it tried to change direction and escape, and the
shifting of the navigation lights of the suited
chasers as they closed in on it with the
semi-electronic vast net in which they planned to
enclose and capture it.

From the distance at which he first saw it,
the bat looked to Johnny like nothing so much as a
rippling gossamer handkerchief, some five
kilometers wide in one direction and four in the
other, painted with a rainbow of colors which
flowed and spread about its moving surface like the
aurora borealis, in their flow over the dark bowl
of the sky in both arctic regions of Earth.

"Chaser twelve-forty-nine, move up to
position!" crackled the speaker in Johnny's suit.

"Moving up to position," he answered, and set
his suit motors to driving him forward. Watching
the distance-shrunken figure swell as he approached
it, the sight brought a heaviness of excitement

to his chest. He had felt this particular
sensation only once before. It had been miles
deep in the Mindanao Trench of the Pacific Ocean,
six years ago, when the running lights of his
sea-home had suddenly shown him what seemed at
first to be only a gray-pink cable or hawser from
some sunken ship, lying on the diatomaceous ooze
of the deep sea-bed.

Then, following the line of it, he had slowly
begun to recognize it as undeniably a tentacle,
but a tentacle impossibly large. He had gone on
following it, driven by a fascination he could not
clearly name, and had ended by illuminating one of
the legendary, great deep-sea squids who looked on

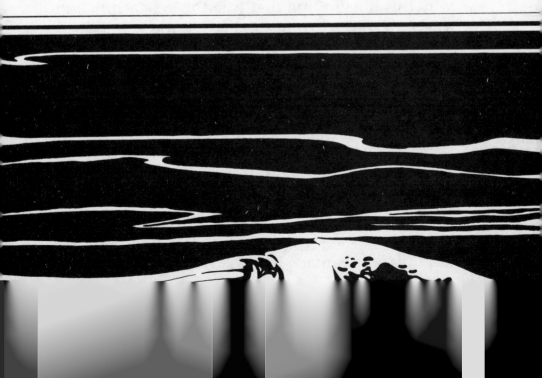

even the largest whales as legitimate opponents;
one of those krakens of ancient mythology and
sailors' tales, who had been reputed to pull down
tall sailing ships to a watery grave.

But the monster squid, somnolent and
indifferent to the mosquito-like flitting of the
small sea-home about it, had radiated to Johnny
then, along with its impression of power and
mightiness, only an animal predator's ruthlessness
and animal savagery. There was no such feeling
emanating from the space bat, now. This greater
creature of the void impressed him in this moment
only with a strange feeling of beauty and wild
freedom, coupled with an inability to understand
why this small thing that was the spaceship, and
these even tinier things that were the suited human
hunters, should wish to trouble it.

Now, moving swiftly to the capture net, headed
for his position on its outer rim, Johnny felt the
velvet living depths all about him pressing in on
him with a power many times that which he had felt
on board. This was not Earth. Nor was it that
little fragment of pseudo-Earth that men had made
out of metal and carpeting and glass and called a
ship. This was the ultimate reality that was the
universe, casting the special unreality of one
little planet's surface into insignificant contrast.
Out here was another place—a place where the

space bat belonged, and it could be that humans like
himself did not.

   Johnny was almost to the rim of
the net and his position on one of the
generator rods, which produced a
fabric of force lines that, out here
where there was no atmosphere, would be more
effective in restraining the bat than cables of
steel. Johnny reached his rod and closed two of
the mechanical hands of his globe-shaped spacesuit
upon it. Activating the rod, he began to move off
at an angle with it, fitting the lines of force it
now projected into relationship with the
other lines being projected by the generators of
the chasers on either side of him.

   Section by section, as more chasers came up
to take control of their individual rods, the net
of force lines wove itself into existence, and
then, complete, began at a signal from the capture
officer to move in about the bat.

   It felt them coming. Plainly, it sensed their
approach, although there was no way to tell how,
for it was only a mist-thin web of molecules with
no visible eyes, or ears or other organs of
detection. It writhed more actively in its airless
universe that had always until now been free of
attackers. A faint drift, like a sparkle of
stardust, seen for a second off one edge, signalled

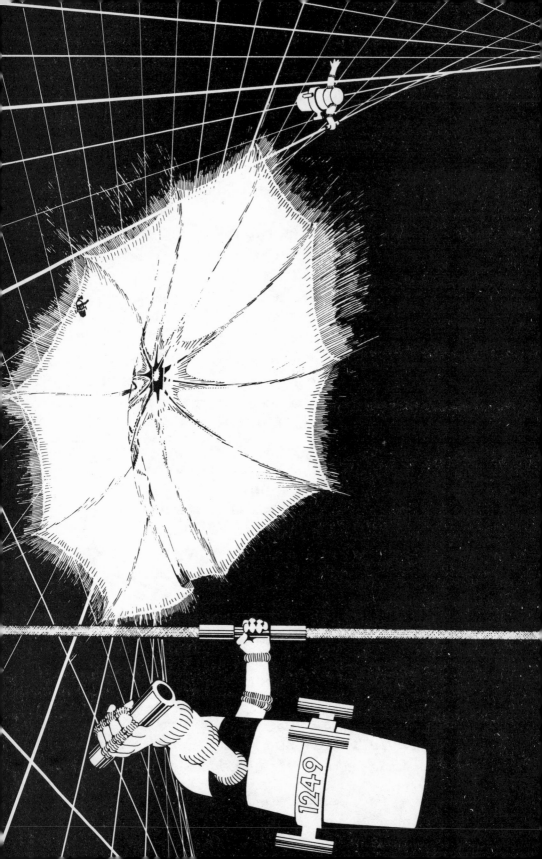

its throwing off some of its bodily mass in an
effort to accelerate away from the metal-suited
chasers and the net of bright force-lines.

But it was no use. Swiftly—seemingly more
and more swiftly as they came closer and closer,
the spacesuited humans and the net surrounded and
closed upon it, the net swirled about it, several
times larger than even the bat itself . . . and closed.

It was trapped. Held. Captured.

For a moment more after it found that there
was no longer hope of escape, it flared and burned
with a racing tide of brilliant colors. Then,
before the eyes of Johnny and all the others on
the net, it began to die.

Its colors flickered and faded. Its frantic
rippling slowed and stopped. It seemed to
contract, to fall in on itself, to shrink and decay
into a lightless, smaller version of itself. In the
suits, Johnny and the other sea-born cadets felt
its dying, felt its life dwindling like a guttering
candle, going away and away from them until it was
only a faint, glowing spark—and then even that
spark was gone.

There was no more light, no color left—only
a drifting, grayish mass without purpose or
value—enclosed in the net.

Chapter 2

"You can't make an omelet without breaking
eggs," the ship Commander said to Johnny. "Your
classmates knew from the beginning that these space
bats died when captured. Of course we understand
that being from the sea you're different. I
suppose something can be done."

He was a short, lean, gray-haired man in
his late fifties with a narrow face set off by
a neat mustache that was still sandy-colored.
There were noticeable crows-feet at the outer
corners of his pale blue eyes. The skin beneath
them was puffed, and the eyes themselves more
bloodshot than usual, after the recent long hours
of duty. He sat, very human and a little
incongruous looking, before a wall picture-scene
showing a section of the towering Yukon Rocky
Mountain range.

"We'd appreciate that, Commander,"

said Johnny. "The truth is, the bat's dying was
more of a shock than any of us expected.
A psychic shock—"

"What you've got to understand, Joya," said
the Commander, "is that there are always bound
to be things like this. I know, there's a damned
general superstition about the military that we're
all very rigid and unfeeling. But that's not so.
I know—we all know—things can't get done right
unless the men and women doing them are
whole-heartedly committed to them. If the people
involved feel they're in a straight-jacket, if
they feel they're in handcuffs, then what they're
doing is going to suffer. Nobody wants it or them
to suffer. Nobody wants you cadets to suffer. So if
you need extra time to make your reports, we
understand. But you've got to impress on the rest
of your people—it's your responsibility as class
representative to impress on them—that getting
this time is an extraordinary thing. It's a
special favor. Ordinarily we'd take a fairly stiff
line with cadets who came along with the excuse of
being upset, as a reason for putting off a report
they should have done the minute they got back to
quarters on the ship."

"Sir," said Johnny. "I've been at the
Academy nearly four years. I think my own
record's a good one, and I—"

"No doubt about it, no doubt about it," said
the Commander. "But you understand me?"

"Of course, sir. But the point is," said
Johnny, "there are differences between those of
us who were born in the sea and people born on
land. There's some things we sea-born react to
more strongly—"

"We understand that. You take small things
to heart. Of course," said the Commander.

"Yes, sir. Only it goes deeper than that,"
said Johnny. "I know how it can sound from the
standpoint of someone born on land—that we can
be incapacitated by the emotional backwash of the
space bat's death. But for us it was an actual
experience—as actual as getting hit in the
stomach. It's not because something died. We're
used to death in the sea. We just aren't used to
death where the dying thing kills itself because
it's been caught and trapped first. There aren't any
cages or prisons in the sea."

"Yes—we know," said the Commander. "All
the same, you tell your classmates that I'm under
a certain amount of responsibility where they're
concerned. Officially, it's part of my job to
see they turn these reports in immediately on
returning to the ship—"

"Sir—"

"Just a minute. Now, it's also within my

authority to give them more time. But I'm going
to be asked why I gave it and I'm going to have
to say the only reason was they requested it, and
because they said they were different. The point
is, for the sake of your own people you have to
understand it's much better for them not to go
claiming special exemptions, not to go parading
their differences. You understand this?"

"Believe me, Commander," said Johnny.
"I understand that as well as anyone
aboard here."

"Well then," the Commander said. He smiled,
deepening the crows-feet. "There's no problem
about giving you the extra time. It's a consideration
within our discretion, so to speak. But the
important bit is, your people have to understand
that this literally is a favor; they've got to
realize that, and not expect some allowance always is
going to be made for them, just because they're
different. Once they get their commissions,
special factors can't come into account this
way—otherwise we'd have a two-value service.
You follow me?"

"Yes sir," said Johnny.

"Well, that's really the only important point,"
said the Commander. "Take your time, but restrict
these special indulgences to a minimum.
All right, Joya?"

Johnny went back to his quarters. There he found Joaquin and a few of the others.

"How was it? How did it go?" Joaquin asked.

"He agreed," said Johnny. "Maybe it'd be better for us one of these times if people like him didn't agree. The worst of it is, he agreed without understanding. He doesn't really know why we want extra time."

"Damn their bloody blue eyes!" exploded Joaquin suddenly. "Couldn't they feel anything? Couldn't they feel it when that bat died? It never did a thing to anybody; and they took it and killed it. They think that that's nothing. Do you know what that says about them? And they think that we should just sit down and write a report about it . . . *'I was out in number fifteen position on number two thread of number eight strand of the net and I trapped it—I helped kill it, and I watched it die, and that is all, sir!'* "

"Calm down," Johnny said. "Letting it upset you doesn't help. It doesn't help the situation for you, or for any of us."

There was a silence in the cadets' wardroom.

"All right," said Joaquin. He breathed slowly and deeply. "All right, I won't let it get me. But I've still got to write that report, sooner or later."

"We all have to write it sooner or later," Johnny said.

The days of their return to Earth were filled
with exercises in handling the ship; this being after
all their main reason—the larger, if not the more
important reason—behind the cruise. Their work
days were long, and it was easy for all of them
to put the idea of the reports out of their minds.
It became something they did not talk about.
Johnny had privately determined to write his
report right after talking to the Commander, just
to prove he could do it. But it turned out that
this was hard to do. He had to force himself to
his desk. Still, in the first off-duty hours after
they were free from the duty cycle that had
included the space bat capture, he sat down in his
cabin and turned on his printer.

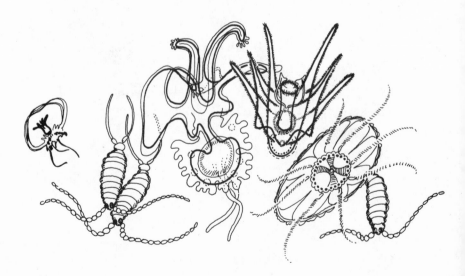

Home from the Shore

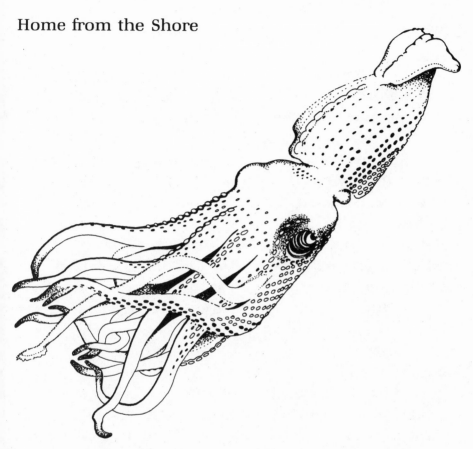

But what he found himself writing was not so
much a report as a White Paper, a policy
statement in which he wrote about the fact that
life—all life—had to be understood and respected
or else no form of life would survive. He drew
analogies from the sea. It was the only place he
had to draw analogies from, out of the endless deep
waters and all the creatures there from the
smallest plankton to that same great deep sea squid
he had seen and remembered ever since. He finished
the report during his second set of off-duty hours

and stacked it, telling himself he would re-write
it into something more acceptable before the
deadline for its turning in came.

But he did not re-write it. Two ship's-days
before they were back on Earth he turned it in,
in its original form, telling himself that it would
be lost among the other reports, that one such
statement could do no harm except to lower his
personal grade for the cruise; and his grade did
not matter, measured against the necessity of
getting the senior sea-born graduated. Accordingly,
he put the whole business from his mind. He had
nothing to think about now, he told himself,
but graduation.

They landed again on Earth. It was eight
o'clock of a warm, soft night when the low-altitude
transports finally brought them back to the Academy.
It stood, quiet and almost homelike after space,
the windows of its rooms alight where cadets were
at study inside. No landers were on hand to chant
them home; but Johnny noticed one window lit that
should not have been—the window to his own room.

When he got upstairs to the room he found
three of the sea-born waiting for him. Two class
representatives, Will Jakin of the Freshmen and
Per Holmquist of the Sophomores, were on his bed,
which had been pulled down from the wall to
provide seating space. Abner Yoerg, a thin,

dark-haired Junior who was Mikros' backup rep. for
that Class, was seated in the chair at Johnny's
study table.

"What is it?" said Johnny, looking at them.

"Mikros," said Abner Yoerg.

"What about Mikros?" Abruptly, there was a
familiar heaviness in Johnny's chest. He began
to stow his gear.

"He's disappeared," said Abner. "And they
won't tell us what they've done with him."

"Who won't?"

"The cadre—the officers. They keep saying
he's off on some special duty which can't be
explained."

"We've talked to everyone but the General—"
began Will; and Per Holmquist broke in to agree.

"Start at the beginning," Johnny said.

He shoved the last of his gear into storage
and turned around to face them. Abner got up to
give him the study chair and they told him about
Mikros. He had gone off duty one evening and into
Albuquerque to visit some lander relatives. He had
spent the evening with them and left, saying he was
headed back to the Academy before his pass ran out,
at midnight. He had never reached the barracks.

When he had not appeared by morning formation,
Abner had reported him missing to the cadre
Officer of the Day, and been told that there was

no need for concern, Mikros was on special duty
and would return "... in a while."

Abner and the others had not been satisfied
with this answer. In fact they distrusted it entirely and
were alarmed. Now they had been waiting to ask
Johnny to go to the general officer commanding the
Academy, and demand to know where Mikros was.

"It doesn't make sense!" said Abner,
passionately, "Why would they pick Mikros for
something like that? There's no reason for it.
Those—Landers know that as well as we do. They're
hiding something."

The little catch in his voice before he
pronounced the word 'landers' marked a point at
which one of the land-born would have sworn. But
in the pragmatism of the oceans, the younger
generations of sea-people had almost forgotten how.

"You're guessing, Abner," Johnny said. "Something
could be happening here we don't know about—
something that does involve Mikros."

"Something we don't know about—but they do?"
Abner's voice was thick.

"Yes," said Jakin, "and something Mikros didn't
tell any of us about? He'd have said something to
someone about whatever it was—not just gone out
one night and not come back."

"All right," said Johnny. "I'll see if the
general'll talk to me tomorrow."

"Talk to him tonight," Abner said.

"All right. I'll try."

Johnny was still in travel uniform. He changed
to dress greens and went down to see the Officer
of the Day.

"Not tonight, Joya," said the O.D. He was a
lieutenant named Harness whom most of the sea-born
liked, a tall, thin young man who tilted his head
back and seemed to sight along his nose as he spoke.
He did this now, looking up from his desk to talk
to Johnny.

"You can't see General Stower tonight," he
said. "Even if he wanted to see you, he's out for
the evening."

"How soon tomorrow, sir? We could have a
real problem. The sooner I can talk to him about
it the better."

"Yes. I know. Well . . . I'll leave a message for
him now and check again before morning parade.
I'll get you in to see him as soon as possible.
That's a promise."

But in fact it was nearly noon before Johnny,
on special pass from his morning classes, got to
the office of the general officer commanding the
Academy. Stower was in his fifties, a square man
with a brush of gray hair, and an explosive way
of talking.

"Come in, Johnny! Sit down!" he said, swiveling his own seat away from his desk and waving Johnny to an armchair. "What's it this time?"

The question was a ritual opening to all their talks. Stower would know what had brought him here. He answered regardless.

"There's some worry about Mikros Palamas."

"Oh, that," Stower frowned. His eyes went to his desk-top. "As a matter of fact, I've been waiting for you to get back. There's some unpleasant news, I'm afraid. It seems on his way back from a pass into town, your classmate was beaten up. We've got him in the Veteran's Hospital across town."

Cause and effect clicked together in Johnny's head.

"Beaten up," he echoed. "By landers?"

"Do you have any sea-people in town?"

"Of course not, sir," said Johnny, "But I think you understand me. I meant—by lander cadets from the Academy here?"

Stower's face seemed to settle into itself.

"No," he said.

"Sir?" said Johnny. He waited, but Stower did not say any more. "Sir, forgive me, but have the lander cadets who were out on pass that same evening been checked?"

Stower's face did not change.

"Yes," he said, without inflection. "Their

movements are accounted for. None were near where
Palamas . . . was injured."

"I see," said Johnny. "Can I see him?"

"You can now," said Stower. He swung about,
back to his desk and pressed a control on it.
"The doctors didn't want anybody bothering him
until today—which is why we've kept back word of
what happened—"

His aide came through the office door.

"Marnal," said Stower, "will you take Joya
over to the hospital to see Cadet Palamas?"

But when Johnny and the aide reached the
veteran's hospital, they found a mild uproar in
progress at the room of Mikros. It appeared that
he had been demanding to be let go back to the
Academy. The argument had now reached the point
where two military policemen had been sent for to
stand guard outside his room.

"Can I talk to him?" Johnny asked.

"No," answered the physician in charge.

The hospital authorities were not interested
in anything that looked like special consideration
for their troublesome patient. General Stower's
aide phoned back to the General's office; but even
with Stower's intercession, it was still more than
an hour before Johnny was finally allowed to step
through the door of Mikros' hospital room and find
him sitting up in bed there.

"Johnny!" he exploded.

"That's right," said Johnny, smiling. But
the smile faded at the sight of Mikros' battered
features. "How are you?"

"I'm all right," said Mikros. "Our bones
don't break that easily."

"Was that what they tried?"

"They were talking about it—before they got
too busy to talk. The thing was," Mikros grinned
hideously under his bruises, "they couldn't hold
me still long enough. They'd get me pinned down
and then I'd break loose again."

"How many of them?" Johnny asked.

"Four or five—there might have been six, but
I don't think so," Mikros said. "I didn't have
time to count too carefully."

"Do you know who they were?"

"Lander cadets." Mikros looked steadily at
Johnny. "Who else?"

"You're sure?"

"Who else, as I said? No, I'm sure, even if
I didn't know any of them. But I'll know them if
I see them again. They were trying to make an
object lesson of me—they talked about that, too—
so none of us would dare leave the Academy from
now on, for fear of the same thing."

"They talked about that?"

Mikros nodded.

"They started out with a lot of things they wanted to tell me," he said. "But then—as I say, they got too busy to talk much. Johnny, get me out of here."

"I'll check with Stower. Maybe we can get you loose tomorrow."

"Not tomorrow! Today. Now! This whole place reeks of sickness, and death and chemicals and pain. I don't know how even these landers can take it. Don't you feel it, yourself?"

"Yes," said Johnny, soberly. "But I can't get you out until tomorrow, I'm sure. I'll do as much as I can. If they won't let you go then ..."

He stopped talking aloud and switched to hand signals, the silent underwater language of the sea-born.

I'll get you out tomorrow, myself, if they won't, his hands said.

All right, Mikros signalled back, then, *if it comes to that, I won't go back to the Academy. I'll run for the sea.*

"If they don't let you go tomorrow," said Johnny again, once more aloud, "I'll ask to speak to General Stower again."

"Tell him I can identify those landers, if he'll line up the other cadets for me to look at," Mikros said.

"All right," said Johnny, "I'll pass that
word to him, too."

They talked for a while longer, then Johnny
left. On his way out, he made an effort to talk
to the hospital authorities, but no one responsible
would admit to having any right or authority to
discuss when Mikros might be released. He went
back to the Academy with Captain Marnal, the aide;
and Marnal, at his urgent request, got him in to
see Stower again that same day.

"He wants to come back to the Academy, sir,"
said Johnny. "He'd like to come now."

"That's up to the doctors," Stower answered.

"Yes sir. But ..." Johnny hesitated, aware of
how his next words must sound like a broken record
in the ears of the Academy's commanding officer.
"A lander hospital's hard on someone who's sea-born.
Mikros reacts to all the suffering going on around
him whether he wants to or not ..."

"It's in the doctors' hands, as I say," Stower
cut him off brusquely. "I can send a message
saying I'd appreciate his being let go back to
duty as soon as they think he's able; but that's
all I can do."

"Thank you, sir," said Johnny. "By the way,
Mikros says he can identify the men who jumped
him, if you'll parade the lander cadets and let
him look at them."

Stower sat looking at Johnny for a moment.

"He recognized the ones who beat him up?"

"Not recognized them, sir. It's just that he remembers them and he'd be able to identify them again."

"What makes him so sure they were from the Academy? They'd have to be in town in civies and without passes."

"He knows, sir."

"He does, does he?" Stower looked away from Johnny, out the office window for a second. He looked back at Johnny, his face calm and motionless. "We'd want to find any cadets who'd do something like that—whether they're from the land, the sea, or the far side of Jupiter. Find them and get rid of them. You say he can identify them?"

"Yes sir, I do. I know he can."

"And you think he's right? That they're cadets from here at the Academy, over on the other side?"

"If Mikros says so, yes sir."

"Yes . . ." Stower looked away, out the window again. Abruptly, he turned back to Johnny. "All right, then. We'll see about it, as soon as he can come back here. That's all, Joya."

"Yes sir. If Mikros can't leave tomorrow, can I go see him again? I may be able to get him to wait more quietly."

"Of course," said Stower.

Johnny stood up, saluted and went out. Back
in the barracks, after the day's duties, he rounded
up the other class representatives, including Abner,
and told them the news about Mikros. He did not
tell them that Mikros might possibly be making a
run for the sea. Such ideas were best kept private
as long as possible.

Mikros was not given permission by his
physicians to leave the hospital the next day; and
it was not until after duty hours that evening
that Johnny was able to make the trip to see him.

"Good, you made it," said Mikros as Johnny
stepped into the hospital room, closing the door
behind him. Mikros' hands continued his speech,
silently. *If you hadn't come by lights-out,
I'd have been gone.*

It's a good thing I got here when I did, then,
signalled Johnny. He went on aloud. "I've got
good news for you. You're leaving, with me, now."

"Leaving?" Mikros stared at him. "Back to
the Academy?"

"That's right," Johnny said. "Stower talked to
the hospital early today; and the order to
release you went out this noon. But you know
administrative red tape. The papers just got
here to your ward a few minutes before I showed
up . . . slow down, Mikros. There's no rush."

But Mikros was already out of his hospital
bed and rummaging in the room's closet for his
uniform. He pulled it out and glanced over it.
It had been cleaned and repaired. He dressed swiftly.

How'd you manage it? he hand-flashed at Johnny
as he pulled his jacket on.

I didn't, Johnny replied. *Stower'd obviously
made up his own mind to get you back quickly. He
wants the whole business over and dealt with as
fast and quietly as possible. He's going to line
up the lander cadets tomorrow morning and give you
a chance to pick out the ones who jumped you.*

"Good," said Mikros, aloud.

"I told him you'd have no trouble."

"I won't."

Since Mikros was returning to the Academy on
orders, official transportation was available.
They returned in the back of an empty ambulance,
on a shuttle run from the hospital to the Academy
infirmary. When they got there, a group of Mikros'
classmates were waiting for them, just beyond the
check-in desk at the entrance to their barracks.
These swarmed around Mikros as he went through;
and he disappeared in the crowd of their bodies.
Johnny, however, was held up by the Duty Officer
as he started to pass the desk.

"General Stower wants you, as soon as you come in," the duty officer said. This night, it was a short, stiff lieutenant with red hair, not one of the cadre staff known to be sympathetic or friendly to the sea-born.

"Oh?" said Johnny. "I'll go over right now."

"You'll wait to be taken over," said the lieutenant.

Johnny looked past the man to the crowd about Mikros, now moving off, disappearing down the corridor and through the further double doors that let them into the barracks proper.

"Yes sir," he said, and stepped aside from the desk.

A single military policeman showed up in answer to the lieutenant's phone call, and with the MP Johnny left the barracks and walked over to the Academy Commandant's residence. They were ushered into an old-fashioned, lamplit library to meet a Stower in shirtsleeves, with a pipe in his mouth and an unsmiling face.

"That'll be all," he said to the military policeman. "Close the door behind you."

The MP went out.

"Well, Joya," said Stower. He was on his feet himself and he made no motion to sit or offer Johnny a chance to sit. "Suppose you tell me about this report business."

"Report business, sir?"

Johnny stared at the officer. It was beyond common sense that he had been escorted here by a guard because of the report he had written on the unsuccessful attempt to capture the space bat.

"I think you know what I'm talking about." Stower's teeth clamped down hard on his pipe. "All those reports you cadets from the sea wrote after the training cruise—the reports you asked the commander for special permission to turn in late."

"Yes sir—but I still don't understand, sir," Johnny said. "We did get the permission; but I think everyone turned his report in well within the extended deadline."

"You know they did," said Stower. His eyes glittered in the lamplight like highly polished brass buttons on some stiff and ancient uniform. "Who organized it? Was it you?"

"Sir," said Johnny. "I repeat, I don't understand."

Stower walked close to him and stared up into his eyes.

"By God," said Stower, softly, "if you don't, who does, then?"

His voice came back once more to a conversational level.

"Do you know what was in the report anyone beside yourself turned in?"

"No sir."

"Then I'll tell you," said Stower. "They all
said the same thing, almost with the same words all
the way through, as yours did. Are you trying to
tell me that wasn't arranged?"

Johnny thought suddenly of the criticism, and
the argument against attempts to capture the bats,
that had filled his own report. There was an
lost feeling inside him.

"No sir . . ." he shook his head. "No one
arranged anything. I assure you. What you tell
me . . . it's hard to believe."

"*You* can't believe it?" Stower gave a short
grunt of a laugh. "Well, it's happened! And how
could it happen unless all of you planned it?"

Johnny stood silent, his mind spinning.

"Well, sir . . ." he began, slowly, after a second.

"Damn it!" exploded Stower, "you're not going
to try to tell me it could be done without
agreement by all of you?"

"Yes sir, I am," said Johnny. "You see, the
sea people—"

"Now, by God! I've had this sea-people
business, and had it, until I'm full up on it!"
snapped Stower. "Whenever you people do anything
you shouldn't, the excuse is always that you're
none of you to blame, because the way you were
brought up in the sea made you do it. There's no
regulation, there's no duty, you can't shove aside

just by pleading your difference from the rest of us.
Well, there's got to be a limit to that and this
time you've exceeded it! Do you know what you,
all of you, did with those reports? You made a
massive, unanimous, political protest against
something that's vital to our development of space!
How can I cover up something like that?"

"You don't have to, sir," said Johnny. "Why
don't you just pass the results on to the
Department of Space with my assurance that it was
an instinctive unanimity, and ask them if they
wouldn't like to reexamine the business of capturing
space bats in the light of it."

Stower's eyes remained changed.

"That might get me off the hook," he said,
his voice suddenly emptied of emotion. "It won't
get the rest of you off."

"We shouldn't have to apologize for anything
that's an honest reaction," Johnny said. "If they
question us, we'll admit how we felt. The truth
of the matter is, sir, trying to catch one of those
bats to study it is a dead end. If we keep trying
from now to doomsday, the bats we catch will always
choose to die once they're captured. The
whole thing's wrong—and useless. It ought to be
stopped; and any one of us would be glad to tell
anyone that, if we're asked."

"I suspect you will be," Stower said.

Johnny watched him closely. When the
general said nothing more for several seconds,
Johnny spoke again.

"Sir," he said. "Was something else
concerning you?"

"Not something else," said Stower. "I've
only got your word for it that those reports
weren't an organized effort. Tomorrow, I've agreed
to line up the cadets who don't come from the sea
and let your classmate pick out those he says
attacked him—and I'll only have his word for it
that they're the ones. You know, Joya, there's a
limit to how far we can go to accommodate
you and the others like you, a limit to the amount
of things I can do to the other cadets and to
the military structure of this Academy; and I
rather think we've finally gone beyond it."

"I don't follow you, sir."

"Follow this, then. I'm going to hold that
parade tomorrow as promised. Palamas can go
down the lines and look the other cadets over.
But all that's going to happen to any of the
people he picks out is that we'll look into them.
Unless there's other evidence, solid evidence, to
prove that those particular cadets were off-Academy
without permission and beat him up, nothing's
going to happen to them."

"General!" said Johnny. "How can there be any other evidence?"

"There'd better be," said Stower. "We're still a society where people are innocent until proved guilty, I'll remind you of that."

"But what you're saying," Johnny said, "is that it's almost a certainty the ones who ganged up on Mikros will get away with it. If that's so, they'll have shown they can do this sort of thing any time they feel like it!"

"Look at it that way if you like," said Stower. "Evidence is still going to be required. Good night, Joya."

"Sir, if you let those landers get away with this, all the sea-born cadets are going to be pushed to a breaking point—"

"Good night, Joya."

Johnny stared at the older man. In the lamplight, Stower's face was like the face of some ancient, angry snapping turtle.

He went back to the barracks by himself, without the escort of the military policeman, who had been dismissed to his usual duties. His mind was racing like an engine under full throttle; and by the time he reached his own room, its activity had begun to turn up certain inevitable alternatives.

There was no one in his room, no one in any
of the rooms along the corridor of his floor.
But he could hear a muted rumble of voices from
the floor just below, where the cadets of the Junior
class had their rooms. Some sort of party seemed to
be in progress. He walked down and found the
noise centering around the room of Mikros. The
crowd there turned to greet him but he pushed
through with hardly a word until he came to
Mikros himself, seated cross-legged on one of the
beds of the room as if on an emperor's divan.

"Johnny!" said Mikros, seeing him. Mikros
moved over on the bed to make room. "Sit down!"

Johnny shook his head and leaned forward
to speak in the other's ear.

"No," he said, softly. "Break this up,
find the other representatives and bring them
to my room. Do it quietly. We've come to
the point of making a decision at last, one
way or another."

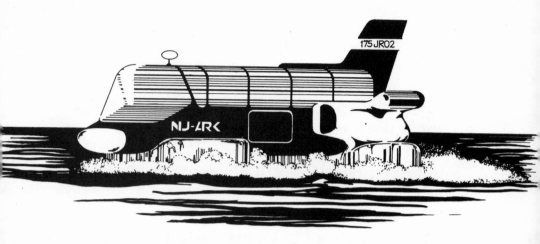

Chapter 3

The hour was about four in the afternoon at
Savannah Stand, with most of the air-taxis, the
day-charter flyers, back in the ranks.
Pilots were hanging
around, talking, and the
smell of solvent was on the air, the water stains
drying back to the pale color of the concrete ramp
floor from the flyers that had just been washed down.
It was, in fact, a few minutes after four.
A gang of the pilots were needling about how the
Nu-Ark was just about ready to split apart in the
air and her pilot never know the difference.
Just then, one of them spotted a possible fare
down at the far end of the ranks. He came up
along the line of parked flyers, a big young
tourist, in a flower-patterned thousand-islands
shirt, hanging outside his pants, walking across
the water stains already fading out like the

cigarette smoke in the sun and looking into faces
under the shadows of the ducted fans as he passed.
He came on down and stopped at last by the *Nu-Ark*
and hired her. He and her pilot took off east, out
over the ocean.

"One to five, in beers," said the pilot of
the *Squarefish* as they watched the *Nu-Ark* shrink
down in the distance, "one of the fans comes off
before he gets back here."

"That's a bad luck bet," said the pilot of
the *Singalong*. "Don't none of you take him up on
that." Nobody did, either.

"You got no sense of humor," said the
Squarefish pilot.

The day was a hot-bright day in late July, clear
as a bell. About twelve miles off-shore aboard the
Nu-Ark the two men felt the motors of both fans
quit, stutter a moment and then take up their
tale again, not quite as smoothly as before.
But the pilot said nothing and the passenger
said nothing. They had not uttered a word to each
other since leaving the Stand. They had not
even looked at each other.

The pilot was sitting by himself up front.
The passenger stood in back. They were in
different sections of the flyer, which was like a metal
shoebox in shape between the fans, and divided
up near the front by a steel partition with a

narrow doorway in it just back of the pilot seat.
The whole flyer had a light flat-tasting stink of
lubricating oil from the fans all through it.
It vibrated to the hard working of the fans so
that anything touched sent a quiver from the
finger ends up to the elbow. Up front of the
partition there was just room for the pilot, his
control bar and instruments, and a wide windscreen
looking forward. In the bigger part of the box behind
was the passenger section, six bolted-down
seats and luggage racks in the space behind the seats.

The racks were forest-green like the walls,
with a permanent color that had been fused into
them. The two side walls had a couple of windows
apiece. All the seats, which were overstuffed
and with arm and headrests, were covered in an
imitation tan leather that still looked as good as
the day it had been put on at the factory. Only
the olive drab paint of the floor had been
scratched and worn clear down to silver streaks
of metal by the sand tracked in from the beach,
which gritted and squeaked underfoot at
every step.

With only an occasional little noise from the
sand, the passenger stood by one of the windows
looking north in the back section, staring out and
down at the sea. To his left, back the way they
had come, the shoreline where the land ended and

the ocean began was sharp and as definite as if someone had drawn it in sand-colored ink. To his right and northeast, from this height the sea was blue-gray, smoke-colored, corrugated and unmoving, stretching miles without end to the horizon, and lost there. There was no doubt about the shoreline. But the distant horizon line where ocean met sky was no line at all. The still, blue-gray waters lifted to the far emptiness until they were lost in it. No one could have said for sure where the one ended and the other began.

    The sky, on the other hand, that went to
meet the sea, was a pale thin blue with only a
small handful of white clouds about thirty miles
off and at twenty thousand feet. Right from the
moment of takeoff, the passenger had seen that
the pilot of the *Nu-Ark* never looked at the clouds.
He kept his eyes only on the indefinite horizon.
Glancing over now, the passenger saw by the back
of a head showing above the headrest of the
pilotseat that the pilot was still at it. It
looked to the passenger as if the pilot was so
used to the sky that he no longer noticed it. He

did not notice the vibration, the faltering of
his.fans or the stink of oil. Likewise, he seemed
used to the look of the sea. But the far-off and
strange part of things that was the horizon drew
all the attention of his eyes.

They were brown, his eyes, the passenger
remembered. A little bloodshot. Set in a
middle-aged tropical face tanned and thickened
into squint lines around the corners of the eyes.
Just then the pilot spoke, without turning.

"Keep straight on out?" he said.

The passenger went tight at the sound of
the voice, jerking his eyes back to the pilotseat.
But the black, straight hair of the pilot showed
unmoving against the tan imitation leather.
The passenger hooked a thumb into the neck
opening of his bright-printed sports shirt. With one
quick downward jerk of the thumb he unsealed
the closure and the shirt fell open.

"Straight on out," he said. He shrugged off
the shirt and reached for the belt closure of his
green slacks. "Another four or five minutes,
this heading."

"Ten, twelve miles," said the pilot.
"All right."

The black-haired portion of his head that
was showing tilted forward. The passenger could
see him finally leaning toward the sea. Looking,

no doubt, for a vee of wake, a squat triangle of
sail, some dark boat-shape.

"Who do you think's out here now—" he began.

He had started turning his head to look back
as he spoke. As his eyes came around to see the
passenger undressing, he moved with unexpected
quickness, letting go of the control bar and
swinging himself and his pilot seat all the way
around. The flyer shuddered briefly as it went
into autopilot. The passenger ripped off his
slacks and stood up straight in only khaki-colored
shorts. They looked at each other.

The look on the pilot's face had not changed.
But now the passenger saw the brown eyes come
to sharp focus on him. He stood balanced
and waiting.

The only thing he was afraid of now was that
the pilot would not look closely enough. He was
afraid the pilot might see only a big young man in
his early twenties. A young man with a
strong-boned body muscled like a wrestler, but
with a square, open and too easy-going sort of
face. Then he saw the pilot's eyes flicker to
the three blue dots tattooed on his bare right
collarbone, and after that drop to the third
finger of his right hand which showed a ring of
untanned white about its base. The eyes came back
up to his face then. When he saw their

expression had still not changed, he knew that
there was one fear, at least, he could forget.

"I guess," said the pilot, "you know who's
out there after all."

"That's right," he said. He continued to
stand, leaving the next move up to the pilot.
Six inches from the pilot's still left hand was
the small, closed door of a map compartment. In
there would probably be a knife or gun. The pilot
himself was big-boned and thick-bodied. The
years had put a scar above one eyebrow and broken
and enlarged three knuckles on his right hand.
These were things that had caused the pilot to be
picked by him for this taxi-job in the first

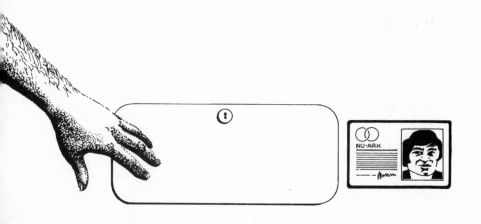

place. He had trusted a man like the pilot of the
Nu-Ark not to go off half-cocked.

"So you seen a space bat," said the pilot
now, still watching him. The name came out
sounding odd in the southern accent; but for a
moment it hit home and the pilot blurred before
his eyes as tears jumped in them. He blinked
quickly; but the pilot had not moved. Once again
he remembered how slow land people were to tears.
The pilot would not have been figuring
that advantage.

"We all did," he said.

"Yeh," said the pilot. "Your picture was
on the news. Johnny Joya, aren't you?"

"That's right," he said.

"Ringleader, weren't you?"

"No," said Johnny. "There's no ringleaders
with us."

"News said so."

"No."

"Well, they did."

"They don't know."

The pilot shrugged. He sat still for
a second.

"All right," he said. "They still got a
reward out for you bigger than on any the rest
of the Cadets."

They held still for another little moment,
watching each other. The flyer bored on through
the air, automatically holding its course. Johnny
stood balanced. He was thinking that he had
picked this pilot because the man was like him.
It might be they were too much alike. It might
be that the pilot had too much pride to let himself
be forced, in spite of the squint lines and
broken knuckles and knowing now what his chances
would be with someone like Johnny. If it was that,
the pilot would need some excuse, or reason.

Easily, not taking his eyes off the pilot,
Johnny reached down and picked up his slacks.
From one pocket he searched out something small,
circular and hard. Holding it outstretched in
his fingers, he took two steps forward and offered
it to the pilot.

"Souvenir," he said.

The pilot looked down at it. It was a steel
ring with a crest on it showing what looked like
a mailed fist grasping at a star.

Two words—*ad astra*—were cut in under
the crest.

"Souvenir," said Johnny again.

The pilot looked it over for a long second,
then slowly reached out two of the fingers with
the broken knuckles and tweezered it between the

ends of them, out of Johnny's grasp. He turned it
slowly over, first one way and then the other,
looking at it.

He said, "Once I would've wanted one like
that." He lifted his eyes to Johnny. "I don't
understand. Nobody does."

"It looks that way to us, too," he answered,
not moving. "We don't understand landers."

"Yeah," said the pilot. He turned the ring
again. "Well, you was the one that was there.
You all go home, you sea kids?"

"It's not our job," he said. "Fill your
Space Academy with your own people."

"Yeah," said the pilot, almost to himself.
Slowly he folded in the fingers holding the ring,
until it was covered and hidden in the grasp of
his fist. He put the fist in his pocket and when
it came out again he no longer held the ring.
"All right. Souvenir." He turned back to the
controls. "How much on out?"

"About a mile now."

The pilot took hold of the control bar. The
flyer dropped. The surface of the sea came up to
meet them, becoming more blue and less gray as it
approached. From high up it had looked fixed and
unmoving, but now they could see there was motion
to it. When they got close indeed, they could see
how it was furrowed and all in action, so that no

part of it was the same as any other, or stayed
the same.

Johnny put one palm to the ceiling and
pressed upward. He stood braced against the angle
of their descent, looking past the bunched-up
muscles of his forearms at the jacketed back of
the pilot and the approaching sea.

"How can you tell?" asked the pilot, suddenly.
"You know where we are now?"

"About eight-one, fifty west," said Johnny,
"by about thirty-one, forty north."

The pilot glanced at his instruments.

"Right on," the pilot said. "Or almost. How?"

"Come to sea," he answered. "Your
grandchildren'll have it." His eyes blurred
suddenly again for a second. "Why do you think
they wanted us for their Space Program?"

"No," said the pilot, not turning his head,
"leave me out of it." A moment later he leaned
toward the windscreen. "Something in the top of
the water, there."

"That's it," said Johnny. The flyer dropped.
It came down on the surface and began to rock
and move with the ceaseless motion of the waves.
The ducted fans were unexpectedly still. Their
thrumming had given way to a strange silence
broken by the slapping of the waves against the
flyer's underbody and small creakings of metal.

"Well, look there!" said the pilot.

He leaned forward, staring out through the windscreen. The flyer had become surrounded by a gang of stunting dolphin and seal. A great, swollen balloon of a fish—a guasa—floated almost to the surface alongside the flyer and gaped at it with a mouth that opened like a lifting manhole cover. Johnny slipped full-eye contact lenses into place and stripped off the shorts. In only the lenses and an athletic supporter, he picked up the small sealed suitcase he had brought aboard and opened the side door of the flyer, just back of the partition on the right. The pilot turned his seat to watch.

"Here—" he said suddenly. He reached into his pocket, brought out the Academy ring and held it out to Johnny. Johnny stared at him. "Go ahead, take it. What the hell, it don't mean anything to me!" Slowly, Johnny took it, hesitated, and slid it back on his right third finger to carry it.

"Good luck."

"All right," said Johnny. "Thanks." He
turned and tossed the suitcase out the door.
Several dolphins raced for it, the lead one taking
it in his almost beakless mouth. He was larger
and somewhat different from the others.

"You going very deep there?" asked the pilot
as Johnny stepped down on to the top of the
landing steps, whose base were in the waves.

"Twenty . . ." Johnny glanced at the gamboling
sea-creatures. "No, only about fifteen fathoms."

The pilot looked from him to the dolphins
and back again.

"Ninety feet," said the pilot.

Johnny went down a couple of steps and felt
the soft warmth of the sun-warmed surface waters
roll over his feet. He looked back at the pilot.

"Thanks again," he said. He hesitated and
then held out his hand. The pilot got up from his
seat, came to the flyer door and shook. In the
grip of their hands, Johnny could feel the hard
callouses of the man's palm.

"It's what you call Castle-Home, down
there?" said the pilot as they let go.

"No," said Johnny. "It's Home." On the last
word he felt his vocal cords tighten and he was
suddenly in a hurry to be going.
"Castle-Home's—something else."

He let go of the doorpost of the flyer and
stepped down and out into the ever-moving waves.

Chapter 4

The ones that had come up to meet him—the seals, the dolphins, the guasa—went down with him. He saw the color of the under-waters, green as light behind a leaf-shadowed window. And he spread his arms with the gesture of the first man who ever stood on a hilltop watching the easy soaring of the birds. He swam downward.

The salt water was cool and simple and complete around him, after all the chills and sweatings of the land. In the stillness he could feel the slow, strong beating of his own heart driving the salt blood throughout his body. He felt cleaned at last from the dust and dirt of the past four and a half years. He felt free at last from the prison of his clothing.

Down he swam, his heart surging slowly and strongly. Around him, a revolving circus act of underwater, free-flying aerialists leaped and

danced—ponderous guasa, doe-eyed harp seals, bottle-nosed and common dolphins. And the one large Risso's dolphin, with the suitcase in his mouth, circling closest.

Johnny clicked fingernails and tongue at the
Risso's dolphin. It was a message in the dolphin
code that the Risso knew well. *"Baldur . . . Baldur
the Beautiful . . ."* The twelve-foot gray beast
rolled almost against him in the water, offering
the trailing reins of the harness.

He caught first one rein, then the other,
and let himself be towed down, no longer pivot man
to the group but a moving part of it.

Seconds later, there was light below them,
brighter than the light from above. They were
coming down into the open hub of a large number
of apartments, mostly with transparent walls,
sealed together into the shape of a wheel. People
poured out of the apartments like birds from an
aviary. They clustered around him, swept him down
and pushed him through the magnetic iris of an
entrance. His ears popped slightly and he came
through, walking into a large, air-filled room
surrounding a pool. The dolphins, the seals and
the guasa broke water in the pool in the same
second. People crowded in after him, swarmed
around him, shouting and laughing.

In a second the room was over-full. There
was no spare space. A tall, lean young man,
Johnny's age, looking like Johnny, climbed up on
a table holding a sort of curved, long-necked
banjo. Sitting crosslegged, he flashed fingers

over the strings, ringing out wild, shouting
music. Voices caught up the tune. A song—one
Johnny had never heard before—beat at the walls.

Hey, Johnny! Hey-a, Johnny!
Home, from the shore!
Hey-o, Johnny! Hey, Johnny!
To high land, go no more!

Long away, away, my Johnny!
Four long years and more!
Hey-o, Johnny! Hey, Johnny!
Go high land, no more!

They were all singing. They sang, shouting
it, swaying together, holding together, laughing
and crying at the same time. The tears ran down
their clean faces.

Johnny felt the arms of those closest to
him, hugging him. Those who could not reach to
hold him, held each other. The song rose, chanted,
wept. It would be one of his lean cousin's songs,
made up for the occasion of his homecoming. He
did not know the words. But as he was handed on,
slowly from the arms of one relative or friend
to the next, he was caught up, at last, in the
music and sang with the rest of them.

He felt the tears running down his own
cheeks, the easy tears of his childhood. There
was a great feeling in the room. It was the
nous-nous of his people, of The People, the People
of the Sea in all their three generations. He
was caught up with them in the moment now and sar
and wept with them. They were moved together in
this moment of his returning, as the oceans
themselves were moved by the great currents that
gave life and movement to their waters. The
roadways of the seal, the dolphin, and now the
roadways of his people. The Liman, the Kuroshio,
the Humbolt Current. The Canary, the Gulf Stream
in which they were now this moment drifting north.
The Labrador.

For four years he had been without this
feeling. But now he was Home.

Gradually the great we-feeling of the People
in the room relaxed and settled down into a spirit
of celebration. The song of his homecoming
shifted to a humorous ballad—about an old man/
who had a harp seal/ which wouldn't get out of his
bed. Laughter crackled among them. Long-necked
green pressure bottles and a variety of marinated
tidbits of seafood were passed from hand to hand.
The mood of all of them settled into cheerfulness,
swung at last to attention on Johnny. Quiet

welled up and spread around the pool, quenching
other talk.

Sitting now on the table that his cousin
Patrick with the banjo had vacated, he noticed
their waiting suddenly. He had his arm around
the shoulders of a round-breasted, brown-haired,
slight young woman who sat leaning against
him on the table, her head in the hollow of his
shoulder. Her name was Sara Light and
he had been looking down at her without talking,
trying to see what difference four years had made
in her. He saw something, but he could not put
his finger on just what it was. Like all the
sea-people, she was free; although he wondered if
the landers had appreciated the difference between
that, and their own legal ways, when they had set
all the Cadets from the sea down as unmarried.
But still, she was free; and he had not even been
certain that he would find her still here with
his family and friends' Group when he came back.

She sat up and moved aside now, to let him
sit up. Her eyes glanced against his for a moment
and once more he thought he saw a new difference
between her now and the girl she had been when
he saw her last—the person he remembered. But
what it was, still stayed hidden to him. He
turned and looked out at the people. They were

all quiet now, sitting on chairs or hassocks or
cross-legged on the floor and looking at him.

"I suppose you've all heard it on the news,"
he said.

"Only that it was something about the space
bats," said the voice of Patrick beneath him.
Johnny leaned forward and peered over the edge
of the table. Patrick sat cross-legged there, the
banjo upright between his knees with the long
neck sloping over his shoulder, his head
leaning against it with the edge pressing into his
cheek. He winked up at Johnny. The wink was the
same wink Johnny remembered, but it put creases
in Patrick's lean face he had never seen there
before. Without warning, Patrick's face looked
as it had been on the jacket of a tape of
Patrick's Moho Symphony, in a music department
ashore. At the time Johnny had thought the picture
was a bad likeness.

He winked back and straightened up.

"The space bats were the final straw," he
said. "That's all, actually."

"Were they big, Johnny?"

It was a child's voice. Johnny looked and
saw a boy seated cross-legged almost at the foot
of the table, his eyes full open, his lips a
little parted, all his upper body leaning forward.
He was one who had evidently been born into the

Joya Group since Johnny left. Johnny did not
know his name.

"The one I saw would have weighed very
little down here on Earth." He spoke to the boy
as he would have spoken to any of the rest,
regardless of age. "But—it was four to five
kilometers across."

The boy drew in so deep a breath his
shoulders lifted. When he let it out again his
whole body shuddered.

"Five kil*om*eters!" he whispered.

"Yes," said Johnny, remembering. "It was
like a silver curtain waving in the current of an
off-shore tide. That's how it looked to me."

"You helped catch it?" said Emil Joya, who
was an uncle both to Johnny and his cousin Patrick
with the banjo.

Johnny looked up.

"Yes," he said. "They took our senior class
of the sea people out beyond Mars." He hesitated
a second. "We were told it was something we'd be
required to do as space officers some day. It's
part of a project to find out how the space bats
travel between the stars, if they do. And how
to duplicate the process."

"I don't quite understand," said Emil, his
heavy gray brows frowning in his square rock
of a face.

"The Space Project people think the space
bats can give us the secret of a practical way
to drive our own ships between the stars at almost
the speed of light."

"And you caught this one?" said Patrick,
beneath the table.

"We caught it," Johnny nodded. "It didn't
try to escape until it was too late. We went
out in special space suits and trapped it in a
net of energy. Then, all of a sudden, it seemed
to understand it was caught. And it died."

"You killed it!" said the boy.

"None of us killed it," said Johnny. "It
killed itself. One minute it was there, waving
like a colored curtain in space, and then the
color started to go out of it. It fell in on
itself. In just a moment it was nothing but a
gray rag in the middle of the net."

He stopped talking. There was a second or
two of silence in the small-Home crowded with
sea people.

"And seeing that made you leave the Academy?"
asked Patrick's voice.

"No," said Johnny. He drew a breath as
deep as the boy had drawn. "After we came back
from the observation cruise, we had to write
reports. We wrote them separately; but afterwards

we found we'd all written the same thing, we
sea-Cadets. We wrote that the space bats killed
themselves when they were captured because they
couldn't bear being trapped." He breathed deeply
again. "We wrote that it would never work this
way. The bats would always die. The project
was a blind alley."

"And then?" said Patrick.

"We wrote our reports separately," Johnny
said, "but the general in command of the Academy
believed we must have gotten together on them,
since we'd all said the same things. For that
reason he refused to follow through properly when
lander cadets beat up Mikros, away from the Academy.
We saw they'd never understand us, or how we felt
about things, so we came away."

No one spoke for a long moment.

"It doesn't make sense," said Patrick at last.

"Not to us, it doesn't," said Johnny. "To
a Lander it makes very good sense. They never
wanted us sea people as people in the first place.
When they asked our third generation to enlist
as Academy Cadets, they only wanted those parts
of us they could use—our faster reaction times,
our more stable emotional structure, our gift of
reckoning location and distance and all the other
new instincts living in the sea has wakened in us ..."

Johnny's voice trailed off. He thumped softly on
the table by his knee with one knotted fist,
staring at the blank wall opposite, until
Sara Light, beside him, took his fist gently
in her hands and cushioned it to stillness.

"We were like the space bats to them," said
Johnny after a bit. "Time and again they'd proved
it to us. I called a meeting of the other class
representatives—I was Senior Class Rep. Will Jakin
for the freshmen sea-Cadets, Per Holmquist
for the second year group, Mikros Palamas for the
juniors. We decided there was no use trying any
longer. We went back and told the men in our own
class. The next weekend, when we were allowed
passes, we all took our rings off and headed as
best we could for our own Homes."

He stopped speaking and sat looking across
the unvarying surface of the wall.

They swarmed all over him for a second time.
But they quieted down soon, the more so as Patrick's
banjo did not join them. When it was still again
Patrick spoke from under the table.

"You were the one who called the
meeting, Johnny?"

"It was me," said Johnny. "I was
Senior Representative."

"True enough," said Patrick. A faint
E minor chord sounded from the strings of his banjo

as if he had just happened to shift his grip lightly
on the neck of it. "That's why the news services
have been calling you the ringleader. But you
didn't have any choice, I suppose."

"No," said Johnny.

"It'll be a hard thing for them to swallow."

"Perhaps," said Johnny. "I've lived with
them four years, and they swallow differently than
we do, Pat. We see and think differently than
they do. We've already got instincts they don't
have—and who knows what the next generations will
be like? But they're not ready to admit the
difference. And until they do, we can't live on
dry land with them."

For a second it seemed as if Patrick would
not say anything more. Then they heard a faint
chord from his banjo again.

"Maybe," said Patrick, "maybe. But we all
started by coming from high land in the
beginning. A hundred thousand generations of men
ashore, and only three or four in the sea. All the
history, the art, the music . . . We can't cut
ourselves off from that."

His voice stopped.

"We won't," said Emil. He stood up from the
chair in which he was sitting. The rest of the
people began to rise, too. "We'll be going to
Castle-Home, shortly. And Castle-Home will

straighten it out with the Closed Congress ashore,
the way they've always done before. After all,
we're a free people here in the sea. There's no
way they can make us do for them against our will."

The people nearest the exit irises were
already slipping out. Beyond the transparent
front walls of the small-Home they were leaving.
The encompassing waters were already darkening
toward opaqueness. By ones and severals, saying
good night to Johnny, they melted away toward their
own small-Homes in the wheel-shape that was the
Joya Group's combined Home.

Johnny found himself alone by the pool.

He looked about for Sara, but he could not
see her. As he stepped toward the iris leading to
the inner part of the small-Home unit, she came
out of it. He reached out to her, but she avoided his
grasp and took his hand. Puzzled, he let her lead
him through the eye-baffling shimmer of the iris.

Beyond it he found not one bedroom, but two,
for another iris led to a further sleeping room.
But in this first area, a single bed was against a
wall, at the foot of which a small night-light glowed.

On the bed, under a light cover with his face
dug sideways into the softness of a pillow that was
dampened by his open-breathing mouth, lay a small
interloper. It was the boy who had spoken up
earlier to ask about the space bats.

Politeness was for all ages among the sea
people. Johnny stepped to the bed and reached
down to shake gently a small bare shoulder and
wake him to the fact that he was in the wrong
small-Home. But Sara caught Johnny's hand; and
when he looked down into her face he found it
luminous with an emotion he did not know.

"Tomi," she said. "His name's Tomi. He's
your son, Johnny."

Johnny stared at her. They had talked to
and written each other across the distance
between them these last four and a half years,
and never once had she mentioned a child. Among
the sea-born that was her right, of course. But
somehow Johnny had never thought that Sara would
not tell him if . . .

He forced his gaze away from her watching
face, back down to the boy. His son slept the
heavy slumber of childhood's exhaustion.

Slowly he sank on his knees by the bedside,
drawing his hand out of Sara's grasp. A chill
ran through him. He felt the heavy muscles of his
stomach contract. In the small white glow of the
night-light reflected from the palely opaque walls,
Tomi slumbered as if in a world remote, not only
from land and sea and all the reaches of space,
but from all things outside this one small room.
He breathed without a sound. His chest movements

were almost invisible, his skin fine to the point
of translucency. The chill in Johnny spread
numbness through all his body and limbs, and his
neck creaked on stiff tendons.

He reached out slowly. With what seemed an
enormous, creased and coarse-skinned fingertip,
he traced the slight line of an eyebrow on the
boy. The brown, fine hairs were crisp to his
touch. An abrupt flush of emotion rushed through
him, burning away the chill like a wave of fever.
He felt clumsy and helpless; and a wild desire
prompted him to gather the boy in his arms and,
holding him tightly, snarl above him at all the
forces of the universe. Wrung and bewildered,
Johnny turned his face up to Sara.

"Sara!" It was almost a wail of despair
from his lips.

She knelt down beside him and put her arms
around him and the boy, together. He clung to
her and the sleeping youngster; and the boy,
half-waking, roused and held to them both.

And so they held together, the three of them,
there in the glow of the night-light.

Chapter 5

"It's good to have you back with us,"
said Patrick.

The two of them with Baldur and Pat's
sea-friend, a spectacled porpoise named Manui,
lazed on the surface some two hundred miles off
the eastern coast of the North American continent.
The sky was blue and clear with only a few
scattered clouds, the day warm with a light wind
and the ocean swells normal; but they could both
feel the warning of heavy weather to come in the
next few days, like a prickling under their skins.
They had gone out together as once they had when
they had been boys, addicted to weeks-long
explorations of the ocean that surrounded them.
But in this case, it had been mainly a search for
privacy that had taken them off. Both knew that
there were things on the mind of the other.

"It's good to be back," Johnny answered as
they floated on their backs, watching the sky,
barely aware of their own small, instinctive arm
and leg movements that kept them half-reclined in
the sea-swell, rocking with the movement of it.
"But you think I ought to have stayed, don't
you Pat?"

"Not you. Not if you didn't want to."

"But you think I shouldn't have led the
other cadets home."

"Yes," said Patrick, simply. "I do think
that. I don't know what it was like for all of
you. But, having gone, I think I would have stayed."

"You were against our going in the
first place."

"Yes," said Patrick. "But after you all
went, anyway, the sea was committed. It's no
solution to our problems with the land to first
agree to join with them, and then abandon them.
There's no answer in just running away from it all."

"I know. But we couldn't stay any longer,"
Johnny said. "It got to the point of being plain,
finally, that there wasn't any hope in staying."

Pat said nothing.

"All right then, what would you do now?"
Johnny turned his head to watch Patrick's profile,
against the blue sky and the green water beyond.

Patrick sighed to the sky and the clouds.

"Go back, I guess," he said.

"Back to the Academy? What would that solve?"

"It'd return the situation to what it was before you left," Pat said. "With land and sea standing apart, things'll never work out, Johnny. We agreed about that once, you and I."

"We still agree about it," said Johnny.

"Then . . . ?"

"No," said Johnny. "The facts are, we moved toward the land as much as we could. We gave, they didn't. But they're like young children. They took everything we gave them for granted. It never seemed to occur to them that they had to give anything back—or even that it costs us to give them what we did. The best of our best generation, Patrick! What if we'd asked that of them?"

"When you deal with a sea-friend, you don't expect understanding from it that it hasn't got."

"These aren't sea-friends. They're us—grown up ashore. They can't be excused for not understanding. If we can make the effort it takes to understand them, they can make the effort to understand us and our ways."

"Maybe it just needs more time, Johnny."

"They've had time. They've had four and a half years from when the first of us came ashore for them."

"All right," said Patrick, "then what are you going to do?"

"What has to be done," Johnny said. "Wait for them to come to their senses. We tried it their way and it didn't work. Now we'll wait for the lesson of that to sink in."

"And if it doesn't? What if they decide to use force against us—all their technology and resources against the tiny amount we have?"

"Then they do," said Johnny. "Patrick, we can't go back to their way."

"Fight or die?" Patrick said, sadly.

"If you want to put it that way," Johnny answered.

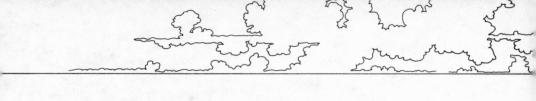

They left it at that and spent the next two days roaming the surface and underwater within a hundred sea-miles or so of Joya-Home. It was a good time, if not a purely happy one—though few landers would have understood the pleasure of the two sea-born in what were apparently only miles and miles of water, empty except for an occasional sea-creature. The landers would have lacked the ability to understand how that water itself was living, charged with varied and fascinating information about where it had come from, what it had encountered along the way, and what in the way of other life forms had passed through it recently.

For a while, both Johnny and Patrick managed
to forget the deadly lack of understanding between
land and sea. They lost themselves in the world
of water to which with every instinct of their
bodies and upbringings they could feel themselves
to belong. But when at last they headed back to
Joya-Home, a silence moved in between them and
the closeness they had been feeling the last few
days broke. They were left, each of them, separate
in his own thoughts as they returned not merely
to the Home but to the problems of the larger
world beyond it. When they came at last to the
spot on the ocean's restless surface that their
third-generation instincts told them was above

the present location of Joya-Home—for the Home
had moved a good two hundred miles since they
had left it—Patrick lifted his head, looking around
at the bright blue sky and sniffing the air.

"Hurricane coming, all right," he said. "Soon."

"Soon," agreed Johnny.

They rolled over in the water like dolphins
and swam down to the lighted wheel of their
destination; and at it they parted, going each to
his own small-Home without further words.

The weather-warning they had felt on the
surface had not misled them. It was the hurricane
season and one big wind had begun its march north
on the day Johnny left the Academy. On the

fourth day after their return, it hammered the
ocean above the Home into spume and dark, tall
masses of leaning water. To the east, it battered
Georgia and the North Carolina shore.

The Joya Home slipped down to twenty fathoms
depth and dwelt there in calm, green-blue silence.
No effect of the howling, furious borderland
between air and water reached down here to the
bright wheel-shaped Home, away up in the middle of
the ocean universe. The People of the Joya group
hardly thought about what was happening above.
In their swim-masks or small-Homes, they breathed
the atmosphere made for them out of the water
elements. They ate and drank of bounty the living
ocean supplied. When they reached Castle-Home
would be time enough to think about replacing any
of the large, complex items of equipment that only
the automatories of Castle-Home could supply.
The land and all its problems might as
well not exist.

Amongst the others, Johnny moved like a ghost.
He was of them but not with them. He told himself
he had been too long away, too long on high land,
and the awareness of the life ashore was standing
like a thick, transparent wall between him and
these, his People.

To those People, and to their third
generation in particular, there was no more a

boundary between work and play than there was
between place and place, wherever the deep oceans
ran. All was one whole experience of life—unlike
the compartmented lives they lived ashore. Johnny
had gone without thinking, the first morning after
he was home again, to the charts on which he had
been working nearly five years before, the charts
showing the movement of the great currents like
the Gulf Stream, at various depths. He had been
only one of the many People engaged in this, and he
found the work far advanced since his last sight
of it. He projected the current status of it in
the display screen of the control area of Sara's
small-Home, that was now his as well as hers and
Tomi's; and he was impressed by what he saw. The
sea-born were very few in number to survey all the
majority of the Earth's surface that lay under
deep salt water, but much work had been done
since he had had a hand in it.

In the computer file were a large number of
reports that had been sent to him after he had
left and before those reporting had realized that
someone else would have to translate these into
knowledge expressed on the current charts. Many
of those reports would be out of date now, handled
by other workers on the project about the world;
but Johnny started to go through them to winnow
out what still might be useful.

It was a work that had fascinated him once.
But now he discovered it had lost part of its power
to hold him—as Sara's work with the temperature
levels in the Gulf Stream would at this moment
be holding her. Experience with the land
beyond the sea and the space beyond both land and
sea had made Johnny someone who could not lose
himself in this former work—as all around him
were losing themselves in theirs.

Truly, he was the odd member of the

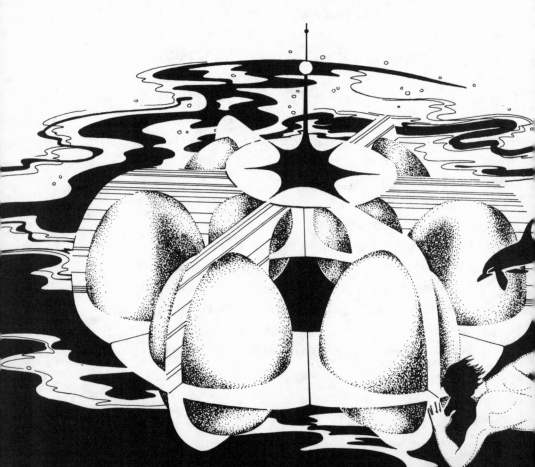

community, though the others as yet had not
seemed to suspect it. Restlessly, on the second
day of the storm, Johnny left his work and went
out to roam the other small-Home units. Entering
the water, just outside his small-Home, he had to
detour around the crowd of young bodies at play.
Among them he caught a glimpse of Tomi. The
boy was so intent on the underwater group chase
going on that he did not even see his father passing,
less than the width of a small-Home away. Johnny
felt himself nuzzled, and turned to see that
Baldur had joined him.

"Not now," he told the dolphin, giving the
hand signal that said he would not be leaving the
area of the Home. He swam on and entered one of
the community small-Homes that operated as
everything from lounges to laboratories.

The one he had entered was currently acting
as a study area for a research group examining
piles of different dried seaweeds. Faces looked
toward him as he entered.

"Hello, Johnny," the workers said in several
different voices, tempos, and times.

They went back to their work. He walked
through and found himself in a biochemical
laboratory where a brief glance and a smile was
all the workers there had time to spare for him.
He went on to prowl the whole of Joya Home and
it was the same everywhere. The adults were all
at their self-chosen occupations. The younger
generation were lost in play. Patrick was not
about and Sara, with others, would be a thousand
fathoms down measuring her temperature differences.
He, alone, was a ghost at the feast.

Saddened, he went out and swam off, away
from the Home, without Baldur, to think things out.
Either one of two things had to be true, he told
himself, moving through the underwater. Either
he was wrong and the land, with all the trouble
it implied, could be safely forgotten. Or he was

right—and all of the others in Joya Home were
wrong in thinking that the land could be
ignored. If the life they loved was to continue in
the sea, then the situation on the shore had to
be dealt with. They could not turn their backs
on the problems there—the overpopulation, the
hunger and the need for other worlds to provide
living space. They could no longer ignore the way
in which the land had ceased to grow, had gone
instead into what was almost a backward movement
toward savagery and decay.

He could not be wrong. He could not be
wrong because not only he, but the other Cadets,
had experienced that savagery and decay ashore.
The land had not only not understood the needs
and the growth of the people in the sea, as they
had not understood the space bats, they had not
been able to see that their ways led only down
a blind alley to racial death. What good would
it do them to take over all the seas, or finally all
the planets they could use, if they were to
continue to remain blind to the larger spectrum
of life and sensation, that stirred in the
sea-people and ran like a rainbow of colors
through the living fabric of the space bats?

And, that being the case, what good did it do
for the sea-people to lose themselves in the seas
as they had always known them, ignoring the storm

ashore as they now ignored the meteorological storm overhead. The road to survival led to conflict with the land—unless the land would learn from the sea. And they would not. They had proved that. The storm of war would leave the safe and distant surface outside the lives of the sea-born and come down among them. They had no choice, because the land was wrong, and the sea must fight or die if the human race was to survive.

And he, who was aware of this, could not make his own people aware of it also.

He turned back finally to the Joya Home. Coming into his own small-Home, he stepped through the iris into the main room and checked himself just in time, overhearing the voices of Patrick and Sara coming from the next of the two inner rooms.

"It's up to you," Patrick was saying.

"Me? In what way?" asked Sara's voice.

He took a step to his right and was able to see through the open iris to the adjoining room. The two of them stood quite alone, facing each other beside a desk piled with notes on which Sara must just have been working. Patrick stood tall, a little bent-shouldered and concerned above the shorter figure of Sara; and Sara had an unhappy look on her face.

Johnny stepped back around the corner of the iris entrance. He was about to leave the small-Home again, when it registered on him that he was the subject of their conversation; and he checked, listening; feeling like a thief in the night for doing so—but doing so.

"Talk to him." It was Pat's voice.

"What about?" Sara said.

"You know what about. About his responsibility to the sea-people. You and I are the only ones who can talk to him. The others only think of taking care of him and doing what he says."

"Yes, and he doesn't know it."

"Of course he doesn't know it. He's never really understood how he leads them. He doesn't understand how blindly they follow him."

"He could look."

"How, Sara? He hasn't got our point of view. He's the one person in the world who's inside Johnny Joya. From where he stands everything he does looks like dull common sense, so he thinks it's the common sense of it that makes other people agree with him. He doesn't know it's what he is, the different sort of person he's always been, and how that's marked him and made other people trust him instinctively."

"It doesn't matter. He's still got to see himself as he is."

"Can you see yourself as you really are?
Can I? Can anybody? Johnny's as limited that way
as anyone else; and it happens he sees himself as
a cut-down version of what he really is. So he
thinks he's being right, when he's really only
being charismatic. And he can't understand it
any other way. So we have to tell him, Sara, you
and I—because there's no one else can reach him
the way we can. We've got to make him see himself
so he can break down and face the fact he's wrong
to separate us from the land, this way."

She sighed.

"Maybe he's not wrong," she said, wearily.
"Maybe we are. Anyway, how can I
tell him, Patrick?"

"It has to be you or I. You and I are the only ones
who understand him—and there's no one else
but us he'd believe it from. I've tried and I
haven't got through to him. So you've got to
try now."

There was silence from Sara.

"All right," said the voice of Patrick. "Think about
it anyway, and I'll talk to you again later . . ."

Patrick's voice was moving towards the iris
as it ended its sentence. Johnny turned swiftly
and left before he could be discovered.

There was a new sadness in him that he could
do nothing about. He had sensed from the moment

of homecoming that there was something making
Sara unhappy. It had been there to be felt in
her, like a gaping rent in an otherwise perfect
piece of fabric. In the first few seconds he had
heard her talking with Patrick—and this, he now
admitted to himself, was the reason he had stood
back and listened—he had thought that what they
spoke about was this same unhappiness of hers;
and he would finally find out what it was.

But that had not been the topic. Now he
had two worries instead of one. Johnny's throat
tightened painfully. He had given Sara a number
of opportunities to bring her concern up to him,
by herself. But she had refused to take advantage
of any of them. In all other ways, she was the
same as ever, equally tender, equally loving. But
she would not speak of whatever silent grief or
anger was gnawing at her. Plainly, whatever it
was, it had something to do with Tomi. She had
never explained why she had not told him about
Tomi; and the boy did not call him Daddy,
but Johnny.

On the fourth morning a call came to rescue
him from his personal problems. It was a phone
call from Chad Ridell, Chief of Staff of the
North Atlantic's Castle-Home, one of ten such
undersurface metropolises that cruised the
seawaters of the world. Atlantic Castle-Home was

nearest Joya-Home's present position, only about four hundred miles north of where Joya-Home drifted now.

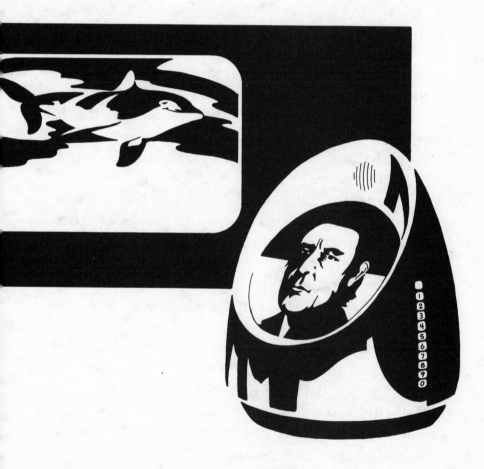

"This time," Chad said to Johnny, "we're going to have to form a council to talk to the Closed Congress."

Chad was second-generation. His lean,
fifty-four year old face had lines more suited
to someone of the first generation. "They're as
worked up ashore," he said, "about you Cadets
going home as they were about keeping the
whaling industry. Maybe more. The other
Castle-Homes have delegated ours to speak for all.
I thought we'd eventually have elections, with
each ten Homes electing a representative. But for
now, I'm simply bespeaking about twenty or so
people I think are pretty sure of being elected."

"Patrick, you mean?" said Johnny.

"For one," said Chad. "Because his music's
made him known and respected on shore. You, for
one of the representatives of the Cadets."

Johnny nodded.

"You'll come as quickly as you can, Johnny?"

"Yes. Patrick too. I'm sure. All of us,
I think," said Johnny.

They broke their phone connection and Johnny
went to tell the others. Within an hour, the
Joya Home was beginning to break into the
small-Home sections that made it up. Each
small-Home sent an electric current through its
outer shell, and the plastic of that shell
"remembered" a different shape, changing into
an outline like that of a supersonic aircraft.
Together, the fleet of altered small-Homes

turned north at a speed of ninety knots, under
the thrust of individual drive units that used a
controlled hydrogen fusion process to
produce high-pressure steam jets. They drove
through the still waters for Castle-Home.

Five hours later, reunited in wheel-shape,
the Joya-Home inched into position and locked down
atop a column of nine other previously arrived
Homes. On three sides the column of Homes, which
the addition of the Joya-Home had just completed,
was locked and connected with three of the other
ten-stacks of Homes that altogether made up the
great underwater community clustering about—and
momentarily part of—North Atlantic Castle-Home.
Johnny, who was acting pilot for the Joya-Home,
locked the controls and turned away from them.

Tomi said, "Why didn't Mommy wait here while
you did that?"

Johnny looked down. The small face, in
which Johnny often found himself searching for a
resemblance to himself, looked up at him across
a gulf of years.

"Her own folk's Home may be here," Johnny
said. "She wanted to find out."

"Grandpa," said Tomi. "And Grandma Light."

"Yes," Johnny said.

"They're my Grandpa and Grandma. They're
not yours." The boy stood with feet apart. "Why

didn't *she* take me to see my Grandpa and
Grandma Light?"

Johnny looked out the wide transparency
before him at the blue waters and the ten-Home
upright columns of Castle-Home. "I think she
wants us to become better acquainted."

Tomi scowled.

"What's 'acquainted'?"

"We aren't acquainted," said Johnny. He
looked back at the boy.

"What's," said Tomi, "ac-*quaint*-ed, I say!"

"Acquainted," said Johnny. "Acquainted's
what you are with your mother."

Tomi looked hard at him.

"She's *my* mother," he said at last.

"And you're my son." Johnny gazed at the
boy. He was square-shouldered, solid and thick.
His eyes were not brown like Sara's but blue
like Johnny's. But their blueness was as
transparent and unreflective as a pane of glass.

Johnny said suddenly, "Did your mother ever
take you to see the corral at a Castle-Home?"

"Unh-uh!" Tomi shook his head slowly from
side to side. "She never took me."

"Get your mask and fins on, then," said
Johnny. "I'll take you."

Outside the small-Home entrance iris,
they found Baldur waiting with Sara's bottle-nosed

dolphin, Neta, and Neta's half-grown pup, Tantrums.

"Not now, Tantrums!" Tomi shoved the
five-foot pup aside and reached toward Baldur;
but Baldur evaded the boy, spiraling up on
Johnny's far side. Tomi muttered something and
grabbed at the reins of the harness on Neta,
who let him take them willingly.

"No," said Johnny. The mutter had barely
reached his ears over the underwater radio circuit
built into the swim masks. If they had been
relying on voice-box communication from mask to
mask through the water it would not have reached
him at all. But he felt it was time to settle
this matter. "Baldur is not your dolphin."

Tomi muttered once more. This time it was
truly unintelligible, but Johnny did not need to
understand the words in this case.

"Our sea-friends pick us, not we them," said
Johnny. "Baldur picked me many years ago.
While I was gone he let you use him, but now I'm
back. You'll have to let him do what he wants."

Tomi said nothing. Letting the dolphins
pull them, they headed across the top of
Castle-Home through three fathoms of water to
a far area of open water where yellow warning
buoys stood balanced at various depths. Neta
jerked the reins suddenly from Tomi and, herding
Tantrums ruthlessly before her, headed home.

"Bad Neta!" shouted Tomi through his
voice-box. "Bad dolphin!"

"No. Careful dolphin," said Johnny.
"What do yellow buoys stand for?"

"Danger," muttered Tomi. He glanced at
Baldur and grumbled again.

"Don't blame the dolphin," said Johnny. "If
Sara were here, Neta wouldn't leave her even for
Tantrum's sake. It's nothing against you. Some
day you'll have your own dolphin for a sea-friend,
and it'll stick with you."

"Won't!" muttered Tomi. "I don't want
scared little dolphins! A great, great, big space
bat, that's what I'll get!"

"Suit yourself," said Johnny. "Well, that's
the corral, beyond the buoys there and for four
miles out. Want to go in?"

Tomi's face mask jerked up sharply toward
his father.

"Past the yellow...?"

"As long as I'm with you. Well?" Tomi
kicked himself forward.

"Let's go in, Johnny."

"All right. Stay close now." Johnny led
the way. Tomi crowded him. Baldur hesitated,
then spurted level with them.

They swam forward for thirty or forty feet.
Tomi gradually forged ahead. Then, suddenly, he
went into a flurry of movement, flipped around
and swam thrashingly back into Johnny.

"Daddy!" He clung to Johnny's right arm
and chest. *"Killers!"*

Johnny put his left arm instinctively around
the boy. Holding him, Johnny could feel the abrupt
and powerful beat of the boy's heart and the
warmth of blood cresting out through his own body.

"It's all right," Johnny said.
"They're muzzled."

Tomi still clung. The warmth racing
through Johnny came up against
a different, powerful pressure that seemed to
spread out and down from behind his ears.

"Look at them," he said. Tomi did not move.
The pressure moved further out and downward.
He put his hands around the small waist and
overpowered the boy's grip, turning him around.
He held his son out, facing the killer whales.

For a second, as he turned him, Tomi had
gone rigid through all his body. Now the rigidity
began to go out of him. He stared straight at
the looming shape of the nearest killer whale
with the open basket-weaving of the enormous
muzzle covering the huge head. Johnny's fingers
pressed about the light arch of childish ribs; but
he felt no shiver or tremble. He was aware of
Baldur quivering in the water at his back; but
between his hands there was only stillness.

The boy relaxed even more. He hung, staring
at the great, dim shape just ahead. After a
second his hands went to Johnny's hand and he
pushed Johnny's grip from his waist. He swam a
few strokes forward.

Johnny felt the hard beating of his own
heart against the pressure in his brain. He was
tense as a strung bow himself; and his heart beat
with the hard, proud rhythm of a man forging a
sword for his own carrying. Without warning he
remembered the striped gold length of a Siberian
tiger lying in his cage outdoors at the zoo ashore
in San Diego. And the small, dancing figure of a
ruby-throated hummingbird which floated from some
nearby yellow tulips, in through the gleaming
bars of the cage. It had hesitated, then,
hovering on the blurred motion of its wings, moved
driftingly toward the great head and sleepy eye

of the tiger that watched it advancing.

Johnny looked about him.

At first there had been only the one killer
to be seen. Now, like long boxcar lengths resolving
out of the green dimness, other ponderous,
dark-backed shapes were making their appearance
without seeming to exert any of the effort of swimming.
It was as if they coalesced, and came drifting
close under some magnetic influence. They
approached sideways. Through the open-work of
the muzzle about the one now drifting, rising
toward him on his left, Johnny could see the
murderously cheerful mouth, the dark intelligent
watching of the eye.

The eye, dark and reflective, approached
Johnny, growing as it came. Behind it lay the large
cetacean brain, and a mind close to Johnny's own.
But that mind was a stranger, self-sufficient.
Staring now into the approaching eye, Johnny
thought he caught there his own sea-image. And
it came to him then that it was for something like
this he had advised the Cadets' return. It was
for something like this that he had brought his
son to the killer's pen.

Very mighty, ignorant of domination, moved
by deep instincts to act to an end unseen but
surely felt, the reflecting eye of the killer
whale looked out on an unending liquid universe

where there were no lords, no chains, nor any
walls. Through this universe only the dark tides
of instinct moved back and forth. For the killer
whale as for the people, now, those dark tides
spoke with a voice of certainty. To listen to
that voice, to follow the path it told of, setting
aside all things of the moment, all pity, all fear
of life or death—it was this knowledge Johnny saw
reflected in the killer's eye. In the movement
of those dark tides there was neither wife nor
child, nor friend nor enemy—but only truth and
what the mind desired. First came survival.
After that what the individual chose to accept.
That was the truth, the secret and the truce of
the dark tides.

And that was why, thought Johnny over the
strong beating of his heart, that it had been
safe to bring his son to this place. His son was
of the sea. In this place was the truce of the
sea, and in that truce he was safe.

"Daddy!"

Tomi's voice shouted suddenly in Johnny's
earphone, in the close confines of the mask and
over the sound of the bubbling exhaust valve.

"Daddy! Look at me!"

Johnny jerked around in the water. Twenty
feet from him and a little higher in the water,
Tomi was disregarding one of the oldest knowledges

of the People—that the quicksilver members of
the dolphin family hated to be held or clung to
by any but their oldest friends. Like a boy on
a Juggernaut, Tomi rode high on the shoulder area
of the first killer whale.

"—Tomi," said Johnny. He felt neither
heart-beat, nor pressure now. Only a wide,
hollow space inside him. He kept his voice calm.

"Uh-huh!" Tomi kicked carelessly with the
heels of his swim fins against the great swelling
sides of the killer. Five feet ahead and below
him, the dark eye there looked like a poker
player's through an opening in the muzzle. It
gazed steadily on Johnny. The great flukes of
the killer, capable of smashing clear through the
side of a small row-boat, hung still in the water.
Johnny thought of the truce, of the primitive
sense of fun to be found in all the dolphins,
the savage humor of the killer whales.

"Tomi," he said, surprised at his own
calmness, "it's time to go home."

"All right." Surprisingly without argument,
Tomi kicked free of the twenty-five-foot shape and
swam down towards his father. For a moment
Johnny saw the boy's legs beating the underwater by
the muzzle where the dark eye watched, and then
he was swimming freely toward Johnny.

Johnny turned and they swam together toward

the edge of the corral. Baldur shot on ahead.

"Tomi—" said Johnny; and found words did
not come easily. He started again. "I should
have warned you not to get close to them.
Killers aren't like dolphins—"

"He's going to be my sea-friend, I think,"
said Tomi, kicking vigorously through the water.

"Tomi," said Johnny, "killers don't make sea-
friends like dolphins."

"Then why does he keep coming after me, Daddy?"

Johnny's head jerked around to look back
over his shoulder. A dozen feet behind them, the
basket shape of a killer whale's muzzle was
gliding through the water. At that moment the
yellow buoys loomed before them, and they passed
through. Here the killer should stop following.
But he came on through with them.

"Tomi," said Johnny quietly. "You see
the iris in the wall there?"

"I see it," said Tomi, looking ahead to the
side of Castle-Home.

"When I tell you to, in just a minute when
we get close, I want you to start swimming for it.
And don't look back. You understand? I want
you to swim as fast as you can and not stop."

The sudden wild clangor of an alarm bell
broke through his words, racketing through the
water all around them and over Castle-Home.

A buzzer sounded in the earphones of their
mask-radio circuit.

"All bespoke members of the Council, this
is Chad Ridell speaking," said the voice of
the Chief of Staff of Castle-Home. "Please come
to the Conference Room at once. All members—"
Chad's voice repeated the request twice more.

"Daddy!" said Tomi, as the voice stopped.
Johnny turned swiftly to him. "Look, Daddy,"
Johnny followed the boy's pointing finger
and saw the waters behind them empty and still.
"My killer's *gone!*"

"Never mind," said Johnny automatically.
"We've got to streak for home now." He caught
up a rein from Baldur and handed another
rein to Tomi.

When the two of them entered their own
small-Home again, Sara was back.

"Mommy! Mommy, listen!" Tomi ripped off
his mask. "We went in the corral with the
killers. And I made friends with one and rode
on his back and he followed us but the bell
scared him—"

Sara's face flashed up to stare into Johnny's.
Her eyes were wide, her nose pinched, the skin
over her cheekbones tight and pale. There was
a white look to her eyes.

"I've got to go—" said Johnny. He pulled

on his mask and hurried out of the small-Home.

He saw he was late as he stepped into the conference room. About twenty of the others were already there. They were seated in a semicircle near the far end of the green-walled room, around the broadcast image of a small middle-aged man, standing, in gray slacks and Lander jacket. Johnny recognized him. It was Pul Vant, Secretary-Advocate for the Closed Congress, governing body of the grouped nations of the land.

Johnny came up quietly and took a seat. His cousin Patrick was among those already there, as were two other representatives of the ex-Cadets— Mikros Palamas and Toby Darnley of the Communications Dome, here at Castle-Home. And Anea Marieanna, a dark-haired woman of the second generation, startlingly beautiful still in her forties and in spite of the fact her left hand was gone at the wrist. She smiled at him across the semicircle, and he smiled back briefly.

"... ringleaders," Pul Vant was saying.

"I tell you," Ridell interrupted. "There are no ringleaders among the People."

"Very well. Setting that aside then—" Vant gestured neatly with his hands as he talked. He had the smooth movements of an actor. "I'm trying to explain to you what the Space Program and the Academy can mean to a frontierless people

ashore." He went on talking. It was an old
argument, one Johnny had heard before. He looked
around the semicircle, noting the difference of
his people from this little man of the land.
Anea Marieanna was not the only one marked by the
sea among the older generations; and in his own
generation the very structure of mind and body
was different. Different from the Landers.
Already they were starting to use the same words
to mean different things on each side. And the
dangerous thing was they did not realize the
difference that was there in their words.

"Now," Vant was saying, "the Congress is
ready to make the same offer. To take you in
as a full member nation . . ."

"No," said Chad.

"You understand," Vant said, "we can't have
six million people without even a government
holding seventy-point-eight per cent of the
world's surface area. You can't do that."

"We've been doing it," said Chad. "We
intend to keep on."

Vant lifted his hands and let them drop.

"I'm sorry," he said. "There's nothing I
can do then, I just explain the situation, that's
all my job is. You know, historically, the tail's
never been let to wag the dog very long." He ran
his eyes around the semicircle. They met Johnny's

eyes, paused for a second, then passed on.
"If the rest of the Cadets'll come back
voluntarily . . . Otherwise, public opinion's going
to get out of hand." He looked at Chad.
"We don't want to declare war on you."

"No," said Chad. "You don't want that."

Vant waved an easy hand and disappeared.
The rest got up and began to shove their chairs
back to make a full circle, breaking out at the
same time into a clatter of conversation.
Johnny found himself next to Chad.

"He talked like they caught some of us?"
Johnny said. Chad looked at him.

"Yes," he said. "A hundred and twenty-nine
didn't make it to the sea. They're holding them
at Congress Territory on Manhattan. It'd have to
be there. The only shred of legal right they
have to arrest our people would be under
international law. Vant told us they may be tried
as deserters."

"Deserters?" Johnny stopped shoving
his chair.

"Why should they?" he heard Toby Darnley,
of the Communications Dome of the Castle-Home,
his slightly shrill voice rising over the others.
"We can't let them put a leash around our necks.
But we can't let them put those young people
before a firing squad, either." Glancing across

the room, Johnny saw Toby's small, square face
was rigid and dark. "What can we do?"

Beside Johnny, Chad sat down. The circle
was formed now. Johnny saw he was the only one
standing. For some reason, following the shock
of what he had just heard, he found his mind
filled by a memory of the eye of the killer whale,
as he had seen it watching through the openings
in the muzzle. The dark eye, hidden of meaning,
and steady. In the same moment something moved
in him. It suddenly seemed to him that he felt
the distant, but actual presence of the hundred
and twenty-nine imprisoned sea-born, as he had
felt Tomi between his hands.

"We can save them, of course," he said. "We
can go rescue our own people."

They all stared at him. The roomful of
people were silent. Though the four walls of the
room barred all about him, he seemed to sense
the eye of the killer whale upon him,
steadily watching.

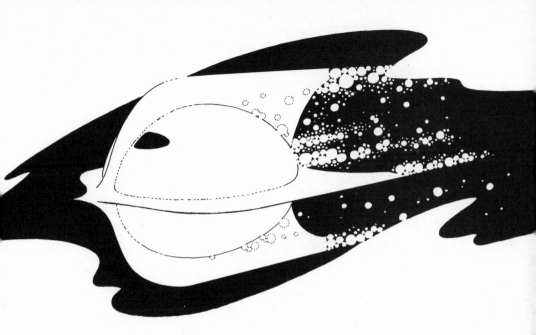

Chapter 6

"Johnny," said Patrick. "You mean take them
back by force."

"Force if we have to," said Johnny. "Chad
said they were holding them on Closed Congress
Territory on Manhattan Island? We ought to be able
to go in quickly, staying underwater right to
the shore, and get them out again without trouble,
before the landers know what's happened. It'd never
occur to them we'd do something like that. They
think anywhere on land we can't touch them.
They really don't understand—even now—what we
can do, so they won't be expecting anything. We
may be able to get in and get our people out almost
without an argument. But, even if it means
trouble—we can't leave them there."

There was a murmur from the rest of those in
the room. Pat looked around at them. He stood up,
pushing his chair back.

"I think you're wrong," he said, simply.

Turning, he walked out. The others looked after him for a long moment. Then, almost as if they had nowhere else to look, all their eyes came back to Johnny.

"Pat may be right," Johnny said. "But I can't sit here and do nothing. If the rest of you agree, I'll go ahead."

Chad sighed.

"All right," he said to the room at large. "Questions from the rest of you? Objections? Any comment?"

There was silence.

"I agree with Johnny," said Anea Marieanna. Her voice was calm and level. "But even if I didn't, he's spent over four solid years ashore with the landers. Patrick hasn't."

She lifted her single hand briefly.

"I know," she said. "Patrick's been making trips ashore ever since he was twelve and the land started playing his compositions. But visiting is one thing, living with the landers, something else. Even if I didn't think Johnny was right, if I had no opinion either way, I'd have to go with Johnny because I think he understands better what's at stake here."

She looked around from face to face, and one by one the others spoke to agree with her.

The sea people could always move at a moment's notice. In an emergency they could almost dispense with the notice. Three hours later, a spindle-shaped formation of separate small-Homes in their craft-shape bored due east through the luminescent blueness of the hundred-fathom depth toward the New York shoreline. Before them, a vibratory weapon on low broadcast power herded the sea-life from their path. Their speed was a hundred and seventy knots.

Piloting the lead craft, Johnny stood alone at the controls. The small-Homes behind held nearly three hundred men and women of the third generation, almost every one of the ex-Cadets who had been in Castle-Home at the time. The small-Homes they travelled in were supplied with automatic controls. The ex-Cadets had explosives, the radio equipment built into their masks, and take-apart sonic rifles and vibratory weapons of the sort the people used for sea-hunting. The element of surprise was on their side, they thought they knew where the prisoners were being held in Congress Territory, and they had a plan.

In the control section of the small-Home leading the formation, facing the empty, luminous waters showing through the transparent wall before him, Johnny felt detached from the speed of their movement. All sound was damped out and there were no signposts to gauge by, only the strange blue twilight of a hundred fathoms down that had so fascinated Beebe in his first bathysphere descent over a hundred years before. It glowed through the transparent forward wall to wrap Johnny in the unreal feeling of a dream. He, the sea, the ex-Cadets behind him—even the destination to which they were all hurtling—seemed ghostlike and unreal.

The sound of footsteps behind him, in the small-Home where he was supposed to be alone, jerked him around sharply.

"Patrick!" he said.

Patrick, dressed like all the ex-Cadets in black, elastic cold-water skins, swim mask and fins, came like some large-footed monster out of the dimness in the back of the small-Home, to stand beside Johnny.

"I stowed away," said Patrick. He was looking out at the depths through which they were rushing at cataclysmic speeds.

"Why? You were against this." Johnny gazed steadily at him. Patrick slowly turned his head, but the apparently brilliant blue was so dim that Johnny could not make out the expression on Patrick's face.

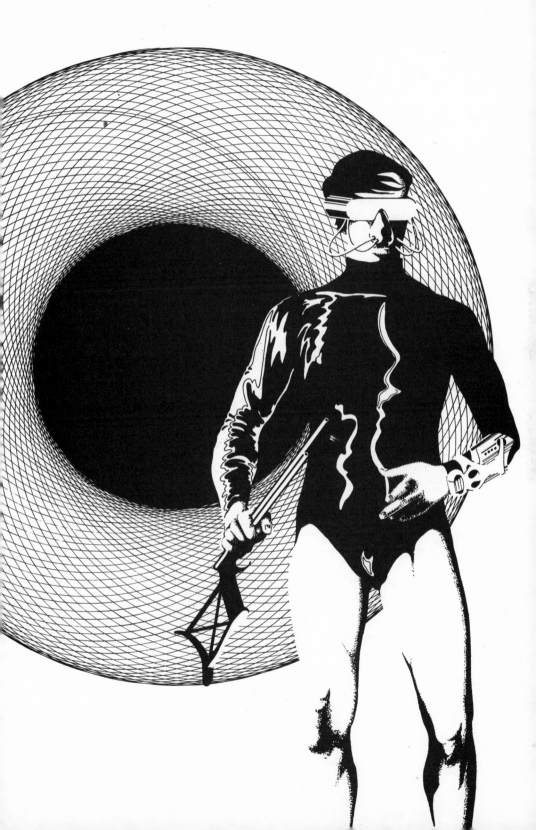

"Yes," said Patrick. "I had to. It's true, you know, Johnny. You're a ringleader."

"Ringleader?" Johnny leaned toward him, but still he could not make out the look on Patrick's face.

"Yes," said Patrick. "Just as you were at the Academy, and before. You decide something on your own. And then you push it through because none of the other sea-born will fight you on it."

"What did I push through?" Johnny let go the controls. On automatics, independently, the craft bored on, leading the formation.

"This." Patrick's voice changed. "Johnny, turn back."

"But we have to do this," said Johnny. "Why can't you see that, Pat? We've already broken away from the landers. We're different."

"You think you're different," said Patrick.

"I know it. So do all the third generation. You know it, Pat." He peered again, unsuccessfully. "You want to make me personally responsible for all this?"

"Yes," said the blur of Patrick's face. "For a war we can't win."

"It's not war yet," said Johnny.

"It's war. War with the land. I wish I could stop you, Johnny."

Johnny stood for a second.

"If you feel like that, Pat, why'd you
come along?"

Pat laughed, a short, choking laugh.
"I knew you wouldn't turn back. I had to ask you
one last time, though."

He turned and walked back, away. In the
dimness, the shape of him seemed to melt, rather
than go off. Left alone, Johnny seemed to feel a
coldness from the blue illumination as if it was
shining x-ray-like through his flesh and bones.

Here, in this moment, it was almost hard to
remember how he and Patrick had been as alike
in their thoughts as twin brothers, back in the
years when they had gone off on their expeditions,
alone with their dolphins and sonic rifles,
living off the open sea like dolphins themselves.
Now, in this new dimness, he could not even call
clearly to mind his cousin's face. What he
remembered was overlaid by the picture of Patrick
he had seen on the paper jacket of the Moho tape
in a music store ashore.

Johnny turned back to the controls, and put
his mind to the coming work.

At a safe distance offshore and fifty
fathoms deep, they halted and clustered for a
final council before going in to the land.

Johnny locked the controls and turned from
them. The small-Homes of the expedition had

welded their changeable bodies back into a single
structure with connecting irises, at a touch of
the proper electric current through their plastic
structure. Johnny went back into the rear rooms
of his own small-Home and found Patrick lying on
his back on the sleeping mattress there, but with
his eyes open, focused on the ceiling.

"Pat—" said Johnny.

Pat's lips barely moved.

"Yes?" he said.

"Patrick, I've got to get together with
Mikros and the others for last minute decisions
and planning. As long as you've come, do you
want to join us, and help?"

"No," said Patrick, still looking at the
ceiling. "I'm sorry, Johnny. No."

Johnny stood looking at him for an
empty moment.

"All right, Patrick," he said, gently.

He turned and went forward again through the
small-Home to the new iris connecting him with
the small-Home adjoining. He stepped through it
and found himself facing Walda Antoyan, already
waiting with a pad of drawing paper under his
arm. Walda was one of the in-betweens, those who
had been too young to go with the third generation
to the Space Academy, but too old to be considered
part of the fourth generation to which Tomi and

those Tomi's age belonged. He was a slim, eager,
sixteen year old with a brush-end mop of coarse
black hair that did its best to stand on end
whenever it was not soaked by sea water.

"Come on, Walda," Johnny said. "We've
got to find Mikros and the other group leaders."

"They're on their way here, already. All
the group leaders are," said Walda.

"Oh?" Johnny said. "Who decided that?"

"Everyone," said Walda. "We've been talking
back and forth on the command circuit all the way
here. Everybody agreed it was easier for the
rest to come find you, than for you to go
find them."

"I see," said Johnny. He started to turn
back to his own small-Home, to hold the council
there. Then he remembered the presence of Patrick.

"All right," he said. "We'll talk right
here, then." He sat down on one of the room's
two hassocks.

"Let's see your drawings," he added.

Walda passed him the pad and Johnny flipped
through it. Walda was a superb sketch artist, in
spite of his youth. Moreover, he was well
acquainted with the Closed Council Territory they
would be going into—Walda had visited an older
second cousin of his, a lander who was one of
the Closed Council delegates, there a number of

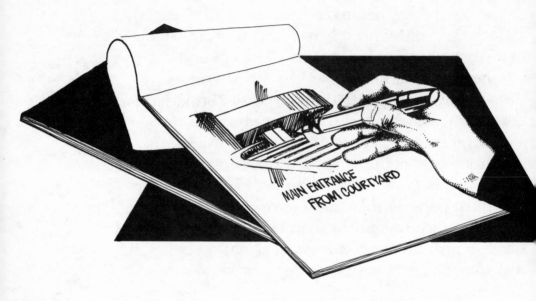

MAIN ENTRANCE
FROM COURTYARD

times. If it had not been for that and his artistic genius, Johnny would have preferred not to have someone that young along. Although, as Walda was technically third generation, it would have been difficult to keep him from coming if he had insisted, in any case.

The sketches were excellent, picturing every step of the way they would have to follow to the old blast shelter beneath the Secretariat building, where it had been decided that the captured ex-Cadets would probably be held.

"Fine," he said to Walda, handing the sketch pad back. "Make enough copies for each of the group leaders to take back to their own people."

Walda went off to make the copies with the equipment in the control section of his own small-Home, just as the first of the group leaders began to come through the iris in the opposite wall of the room.

Of all the class representatives, Mikros was the only other to make it safely back to sea from the Academy; which was unfortunate, since the representatives were not only natural leaders, but recognized as such by the other ex-Cadets. Johnny needed a minimum of two lieutenants he could trust to know how he himself would decide, in case something happened to him, or in case he was not available to make decisions in an emergency. To match Mikros, he had picked an older third-generation hand—almost an in-between, one generation up from Walda—named Eva Loy. Eva had been too old to go to the Academy, but she had been one of the early spokesmen for the third generation, and she was known and respected by all the ex-Cadets.

The small-Home around Johnny was filling rapidly, now. There was a group leader for every fifty individuals in the expedition. Walda came back with copies of his sketches for everyone;

and Johnny waited until these had been passed
around, then spoke briefly to all of them as they
sat, for the most part, cross-legged on the carpet
of the small-Home, listening.

"I've written out the general plan for you,"
Johnny said, standing. "You should all have had
copies of that before we left Castle-Home. If
you haven't, get Walda to make you copies from
some one here who's got his copies along.
Deliberately, I haven't spelled things out. We'll
rendezvous by part-groups of four and five, as
indicated, at points surrounding Closed Congress
territory and less than four blocks away. At
click signals over the mask intercoms—you'd
probably best keep your hand on the swim-mask in
your pocket, so you can read the vibration of the
transmission through your fingertips—we'll all
move together into the Territory, each group on
its own taking care of any problems it runs into
along the way. Don't put on your masks until you
have to. There's no point in attracting attention
until we have to. Once we're all inside the
Territory, everyone but Mikros', Eva Loy's groups
and mine will spread out through the Territory,
except the Conservatory. The three groups which will
be holding the Conservatory have already been told
who they are. The rest of you simply keep
control of the Territory until my group, with

Mikros' and Eva's, have got our people free; and
we can all take off directly into the East River."

He looked around the faces in the room to
see if they were all understanding him. Seeing
they were, he went on.

"The small-Homes needed to take us all off
will have moved into position in the River opposite
the Territory by the time we all reach the
Conservatory," he said. "They'll load up with
everyone and carry us out to the rest of the
small-Homes offshore. Then we'll spread ourselves
out among all the small-Homes, if we have time,
and head for Castle-Home. If something goes
wrong, anyone gets lost, or there are difficulties,
everyone heads for Castle-Home on his or her own."

He paused. They waited for him to finish.

"I've deliberately held the planning our moves
to a minimum," he said, "for two reasons. First,
none of us have any experience with this, and so
I'm trusting you all to reason your way through
any trouble, rather than follow some plans laid
down earlier, which by the time the trouble shows
up may not even apply. Second, part of our
strength and difference from the land is the fact
we're used to thinking for ourselves—and that's
going to make it hard for the land to guess what
we'll do next, if matters reach that point.
So . . . good luck. Come to your group leaders or me

with any questions you've got—now. There
won't be a chance later."

He stopped talking, and sat down.
Surprisingly, only five of the leaders
congregated around him with questions, and three
of these were with the half-dozen who would be
putting together some eleven of the small-Homes

into a mockup roughly the shape and size of one of
the lander deep-sea submarines, resting in the
Brooklyn Navy Yard a handful of miles away.

The planning and briefing completed, they
went on into shallow waters. The Brooklyn Yard
small-Homes split off from the others. The rest
continued together to just off Jones Beach, where they
were to drop all but the skeleton crew which
would take them on automatic controls to
their station in the East River, just off
Congress Territory.

Patrick and Johnny among the others, they
slipped into the water outside their small-Homes
and headed in to shore, dispersing as they went,
so that they emerged at last as individuals, on the
early evening of a hot July day, among the lander
swimmers and skin divers of the crowded beach.

Johnny bought lander shirt and loose trousers
from an automatic dispenser of disposable
clothing in a pullman dressing room above the
beach. His disassembled sonic rifle and swim
mask with its intercom were tucked, out of sight,
under his belt beneath the loose shirt. He
boarded one of the small six-person cars of the
Personal Rapid Transit line in to Manhattan.

The car was empty, except for a young lander
woman in her late teens or early twenties. She
was reading a newstand tape in its throwaway

display unit as they travelled, her narrow,
serious face between its two
wings of black hair
intent on whatever it was
she was absorbing from
the printed page thrown
on the small screen in her
lap. She stirred him
strangely, and without
warning Johnny felt himself
touched by a sense of loss
at the thought that she was
one of those he would never
meet, never get to know or
even speak to, because of
the large forces that
moved them
separately on tracks
that would
never cross.

She left the P.R.T. car at a stop less than halfway in to Manhattan. Johnny continued to the destination he had programmed for the car, two blocks from the Closed Congress Territory.

The Territory covered what had formerly been an area of twenty-blocks, running south from where the old Queensboro bridge had been. It was a show place, beautifully terraced and landscaped, and quite open, its grounds running down to the edge of the river. At midnight, Johnny reached the broad boulevard entrance at the north end and saw Mikros and Eva Loy come up to him.

"All clear?" Johnny asked.

"All clear," said Mikros. His big face under its black hair was grinning. Eva looked strangely calm under the lights of the Manhattan dome. Johnny himself felt a little as he had felt facing the killer whales with Tomi.

"The reports are that there's no one to be seen outside the buildings, in the Territory," Eva reported.

"Move everybody in, then," Johnny said. They went in. Half an hour later, without being stopped, they were all within the Territory, with Johnny's, Mikros' and Eva's groups spread out around the otherwise deserted Conservatory, surrounded by office buildings, that lay before

the Secretariat. The pool in the center of the
Conservatory was black and still.

"What if they aren't in the blast shelter
under the Secretariat Building?" Eva asked as
with Tommy and Mikros they moved toward the
entrance to the Secretariat followed by the
members of their groups.

"We just have to hope they are and we don't
have to search. Where else could they hold a
hundred and twenty-nine people?" answered Johnny.
"But if they aren't, we'll just have to search."
Leaving Mikros in charge outside, Johnny and Eva,
with a dozen of the ex-Cadets, went into the
building and down the regular ramp escalators to
a special old fashioned, mechanical elevator in
a sub-basement. They descended the final
distance in this; and it let them out into a
guardroom filled with Closed Congress soldiers,
half-dressed and wholly unready to fight.

The soldiers submitted without protest.
They were lined up and disarmed. The inner doors
to the blast shelter were broken open and the
captured ex-Cadets poured out.

"That's good," said Johnny to Eva. "Now,
get them upstairs as quickly as we can."

He was turning back to the elevator—when
the dull, heavy sound of a sonic explosion from
above rattled the elevator in its shaft.

For a second no one moved. Then Johnny
snatched his swim mask out of his pocket,
thumbed the controls and spoke into his intercom.

"Mikros?" he said. "What happened?"

Mikros' answer was broken, blurred by the
buzzing of a distorter.

". . . soldiers up in the buildings!"

"Take charge," said Johnny to Eva. He leaped
into the elevator, rode it up, then ran up the
humming escalators to the ground floor.

Through the glass front of the building, he
could see the Conservatory, lush with flowers,
trees and other plants. Looking up through the
foliage, Johnny saw most of the dome lights were
out. In the dimness, the sea people had taken cover
where they could behind hedges and ornamental
trees surrounding the pool. From the buildings on
three sides of the plaza military gunfire was
reaching for them.

Mikros was not to be seen. The springing
of the trap that had been obviously laid for them
had evidently caught him somewhere out of sight.
The ventilation was off; and as Johnny watched,
smoke drifting out of the building on Johnny's
right began to thicken and fog the air in layers
that did not move. An explosion or something
like it had splashed water out of the pool,
darkening one of the terraces as if the concrete

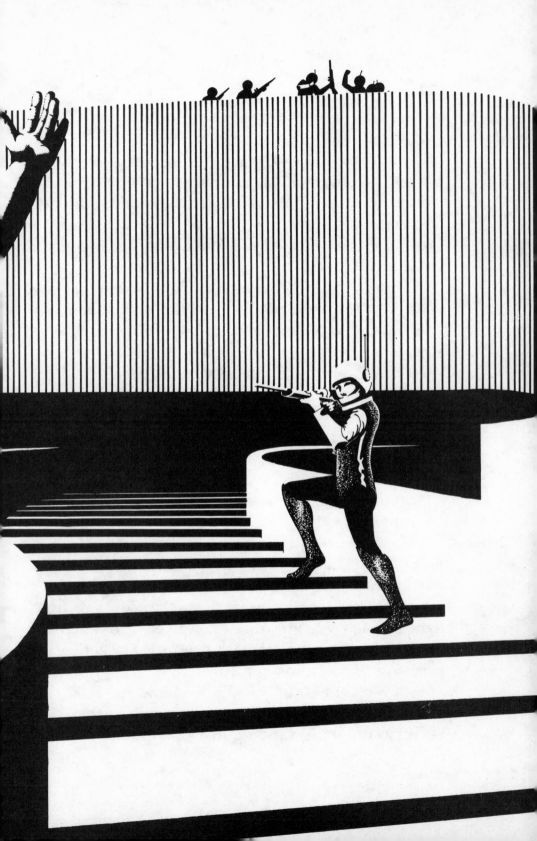

of which it was made was itself bleeding. But of
actual blood, there was no sign; for the sonic and
vibratory weapons that were being used wounded
and damaged internally.

"Yes." Johnny climbed automatically to his feet.
He glanced along the Secretariat's front
and dimly, through the smoke, saw an armed figure
waving to him and pointing aside. For a second
Johnny stared, recognizing only from general
signals about the figure that it was one of the
sea-born. Then he forgot about making an
identification as memory clicked in his head from
the sketches Walda had made. The passageway
down which the figure was pointing, a passageway
between two of the buildings, led toward
the river.

"Follow me," he snapped to Eva.
"Bring everybody."

He ran toward where he had last seen the
figure but it had already disappeared in the
smoke. However, when he reached the passage
entrance and looked down it, the smoke here was
light enough for him to see it was clear of enemy.
He snatched his swim mask from his pocket,
pressing the sending control.

"Everybody out!" he shouted into it. "This
is Johnny Joya! Take the passage north of the
Secretariat. I'll be standing just outside it.

Look for me."

He was suddenly conscious of Eva standing
at his elbow.

"Everybody out!" he repeated to her, and
pointed to a flowerbed beside the passage entrance.
"Explosive! There!"

Eva ran to the flowerbed and dropped to her
knees on the soft earth. From under her own
loose lander shirt she fumbled a number of the
yellow cubes of explosive jelly the sea-born used
for deep-sea mining. She scooped a hole and

tumbled the cubes in, pushing earth on top of them.
Sea-people began to throng past, running,
staggering by them through the smoke. Gradually
the escaping figures thinned out and ceased.
Mikros loomed up out of the smoke and stopped
before Johnny.

"Are they all out?" Johnny asked.

"All but you and me," shouted
Mikros, hoarsely.

Johnny, putting on his mask, glanced at the
flowerbed and saw Eva, too, was gone. The
passage loomed empty except for smokehaze.
"I'll be along in a—"

The swelling impact of another explosion
shuddered through the square. Johnny looked and
saw Mikros' lips move, but he heard nothing.
They were deafened. Johnny waved Mikros on
toward the river, saw him leap up, then run off
through down the passage.

Johnny waited. Mikros did not appear.
There was no more time. Johnny turned and ran,
pressing the detonator transceiver at his belt.
Behind him the smoke billowed and swirled in an
explosion he could not hear. He ran for
the river.

"All over, into the water," he shouted into
his mike; but he could not even hear himself. He
felt an unexpected fear. If they could not
hear him . . .

But then he reached the balcony, fifty feet
above the river; and all was going well. The
unhurt ex-Cadets were going over feet-first. The
wounded were being slid down escape chutes of
plastic. The small-Homes were waiting in the
water below. He could see little of this in the
smoke, but he knew it was so. Suddenly he seemed
to hook in on a network of awareness. It was as
it had been when he had stood in the conference
room and felt the hundred and twenty-nine
prisoners as if he held them like Tomi, between
his hands. In this emergency some new instinct
of the third generation was taking over; and they
were all a unit.

"Keep moving," he said automatically. With
his new awareness he felt they had heard him.
Then he realized that also his own numbed hearing
was beginning to recover. A little moving air
off the river cleared the smoke from the balcony.
Only Mikros was standing with him. He motioned
Mikros over, then turned to go himself. Then he
felt one of the People still coming from the
direction of the plaza.

"Who—" he said, turning. Through the smoke
he saw the figure that had waved that the passage
was clear. Then another breath of air cleared
the smoke for a moment and he saw that it was—as
it had been earlier—Patrick with a soldier's

vibrator rifle in his hands.

"You, Pat?" said Johnny, staring. Suddenly it broke on him. Suddenly he understood a great many things. "*You* told the Land we were coming!"

Pat stopped a few feet from him. The rifle wavered in his grasp, pointing at Johnny. Then, with a sob Patrick threw the gun from him, grabbed Johnny and, stooping, threw him back over the balcony. Johnny turned instinctively like a cat in the air. And the water smashed hard against him.

He caught himself, readjusting his mask, six feet under. Below him he saw the small-Homes waiting. He turned and swam down to them.

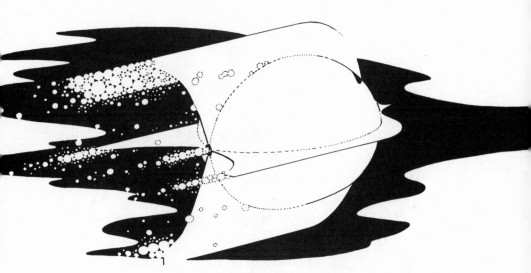

Chapter 7

There was no way to assess the cost of the
expedition until they were once more safely and
deeply at sea. The individual small-Homes waiting
in the river fled each on its own toward open
ocean, with whomever they had crowded aboard
them. Finally, they rendezvoused with each other
eight miles out in the Atlantic and below the
four hundred fathom mark of depth. There, at
last, they combined once more into a single unit
and headed toward Castle-Home.

Johnny walked through the individual
small-Homes in which the wounded and the
untouched had sorted themselves out. There was
a thick feeling of numb disbelief that wrapped
about him like a heavy blanket.
In spite of the necessity of what they had needed
to do, in spite of his own personal effort to
privately anticipate the worst that could

happen, the thought of the dead and possibly
the wounded they had left behind, as well as the
actuality of the wounded sea-born around him now,
left him stunned.

Troubled as the world had been for forty
years, it had not experienced organized fighting
and killing in all that time; and this had been
organized fighting and killing. It had been war—
war he himself had set in motion. Around and
around in his head as he went from small-Home to
small-Home, from bed to bed of the wounded,
the question hammered at him of what he could
have done differently to avoid it all.

Always, the question returned unanswered.
There must have been something he could have
done. Anything would have been preferable to
this. But every time he went around with it
he came back to the fact that he would
have been forced to the same decision again.
Simply, it had been a choice between death and
submission. If they had let the land get away
with arresting the hundred and twenty-nine
ex-Cadets, they could no longer have called
themselves free. And, being what they were—what
their sea-birth had made them—they could not
survive otherwise than as a free people.

And where was Patrick now, back on the land?
What did the landers feel about him, now that

the sea-born had rescued their own? Did the land
know how he had helped the rest of them to
get away . . . ?

Unexpectedly, Johnny's mind cleared a little;
and he suddenly understood the two contradictory
things Patrick had done this day. A lifetime
of growing up with his cousin had made it almost
possible for him to think the other's thoughts.

No more than he could have, himself, could
Pat have given the land the information of where
and when they were coming ashore if Patrick had
known of the manner in which the land would be
waiting for them. When Patrick had seen the armed
landers, when he had heard the firing and seen the
sea-born dying, that was when Pat must have
changed sides again, somehow cleared the soldiers
from the passage along which they had escaped, and
led the rest of them to safety down it. Then, having
done that, he had—as might be expected of someone
like him—refused to return to the generation he
had betrayed. He had stayed ashore instead, to face
the landers, alone, with his betrayal of *them.*

Grief for Patrick stirred powerfully in
Johnny, to blend with other grief for the
dead and wounded sea-born. He paced back and
forth through the combined small-Homes, until
Mikros and Eva Loy came and forced him to go back
to his own small-Home and lie down.

He had not dreamed that he would be able
to sleep. But sleep he did, almost immediately.
A sodden, dreamless sleep of utter exhaustion.

"Don't hang to your father," said Sara to
Tomi, when Johnny was once more back in the
small-Home with them.

"But—"

"Not now," Sara said. "They're waiting for
him in the Conference Room. Daddy just came by
for a minute, and we have to talk.
Go swim outside."

Tomi hesitated, standing on one foot,
face screwed up.

"You go!" said Sara. Her voice had a hard
note in it Johnny had never heard before. Tomi's
eyes went wide and he left.

Johnny watched him go numbly. The Lander
subs had chased them out into open sea. The
decoy they had made out of the small-Homes had
drawn them off. On automatic controls, it had
led the subs three miles deep to the Atlantic
ooze and then blown itself up, taking at least
one sub with it. A Lander sub carried over two
hundred men. There had been more than a hundred
of the ex-Cadets who had not come back.

Riding home after that in the rest of the
small-Homes, those that returned had begun to
sing "Hey, Johnny!" And the song had spread over

the radio circuit from ship to ship until they
all sang. Johnny had turned his face to the
rushing blue beyond the transparent wall of his
craft to hide the fact he could not sing along
with them.

Patrick's voice had sounded again in his ears.
"You're a ringleader—"

". . . I've got to talk to you about Tomi,"
Sara was saying.

"Now?" he said dully.

His real reason for detouring by here on
his way to the Conference Room was that he had
wanted to hide for a few moments. At the sound
of his son's name he shivered unexpectedly. The
dark eye of the killer whale had come back to his
mind. But now it gazed without change and
without pity on the still shape of the young
ex-Cadet he had seen die in the
conservatory ashore.

"I've never told you why I didn't let you
know about you having a son, all these years.
Do you know why?"

"Why?" He focused on her with difficulty.
"No—no, I don't." He became aware, for the
first time, that her face was stiff and pale.
"Sara, what is it?"

"I didn't tell you," she said as if she were
reciting a lesson, "because I didn't want him

to be like you."

He thought of Patrick and the men who
were now dead.

"Well," he said, "I don't blame you."

"Don't *blame* me!" Without warning she began
to cry. It was not the easy, relief-giving
sorrow of the People. Her tears were angry. She
stood with them running down her cheeks and her
fists clenched, facing him. "I knew what you
were like when I fell in love with you! I knew
you'd always be going and pushing things through.
No matter what it cost, no matter who it hurt.
You say things and people do them—it's something
about you! And you just take it all for granted."

He put his hands on her to soothe her, but
she was hard as a rock.

"But I wasn't going to let you kill my baby!"
she thrust at him. "I was going to hide him—keep
him safe, so he'd never know what his father
was like and want to go and be like him. And go
away from me, too, without thinking of anything
but what he personally wanted to do, and get
himself killed for nothing."

"Sara—" he said.

"And then you came back. And he told me
about the business in the killer whale corral.
And then I knew it was no use. No use at all.
Because he was born just like you, and there was

nothing I could do to protect him, no matter
what I did. *My* child . . ." and with that, at
last she broke down. All the hardness went out
of her; and he held her to him as she cried.

For a moment or two he thought the crisis
was over. But she stiffened again and pulled
away from him.

"You've got to make me a promise," she
said, wiping her eyes.

"Of course," he said.

"Not of course. You listen to what I want.
You make me a promise that if anything happens
to me, you'll take care of him. You'll keep him
safe. Not the way you would—the way I'd keep him
safe. You promise me."

"Nothing's going to happen to you."

"Promise me!"

"All right," he said. "I promise I'll take
care of him the way you would."

She wiped her eyes again. "You'd better
go now. They'll be waiting for you. Oh, wait."
She turned and hurried from him, back into the
bedroom. She came back in a second with a tangle
of smashed plastic and dangling wires.

"Patrick left it for you," she said. "He
said you'd understand."

Numbly he took the ruined banjo.

When he finally reached the Conference Room,

it was full of Council members.

"It's war," said Chad Ridell, looking at him
bleakly. "We got their announcement of it an
hour after you landed at Jones Beach—an hour
before one of our gull-cameras picked up this."

He touched a button on his chair. The end
of the room blanked out. Johnny saw a
gull's-view image of the Atlantic surface in the
cold, gray-blue light of early dawn. His
sea-instinct recognized the spot as less than
a hundred miles south.

"Look," said Chad. There was a flicker in the sky, and a hole yawned suddenly, huge and deep in the ocean's face. For a moment the unnatural situation lasted. And then leaping up through the hole moved a fist of water. It lifted toward the paling sky of dawn like a mountain torn from the ocean floor; and a roar like that of some huge, tortured beast burst on the Conference Room.

The fist stretched out into a pillar, broke and disintegrated. A cow biscay whale drifted by on her side, trying to turn over, blood running from the corner of her mouth.

"Sonic explosion," said Johnny. "Big enough for all Castle-Home."

"They meant that announcement of war," said Chad.

"But why bomb empty ocean?" Johnny said.

"Castle-Home was there three hours ago," put in Eva Loy, who was standing close by Chad. "They must have spotted us from a satellite and thought we were still close. We can stay deep from now on, though."

Johnny nodded. Castle-Home had been at a hundred fathoms when the expedition had come back. He remembered what he was carrying.

"No," he said, "even that won't work." He handed the tangle of broken plastic and wires

to Chad, who stared at it, blankly.

"It's Patrick's banjo," said Johnny.
"Pat went in with us. He was the one who tipped
off the Congress soldiers so that they laid that
trap in the plaza for us. He's on their side now."

"But Patrick—" Eva Loy stared at him across
Chad. "Patrick's third generation! He can find
Castle-Home as well as any of us."

"That's right," said Johnny.

"But I don't understand it!" Chad got up
abruptly from his chair. He faced Johnny.
"Why Patrick?—Patrick of all people?"

"I don't know," said Johnny. "He thinks
we're wrong to fight the land. It's what he
believes, I guess." He shrugged his shoulders
unhappily. "Maybe I was wrong."

"You don't believe that," said Eva.

"No, I guess not." Johnny tried to smile
at Eva. His promise to Sara was still strong
in his mind. "At any rate, the only thing that seems
to make sense to me, now, is for me and anyone
else who wants to come with me to give ourselves
up to them." He glanced at Chad. "If they get
what they call ringleaders, maybe—"

Cutting through what he was going to say,
came the sudden, brazen shrieking of the
alarm·bell.

"Missile!" cried a voice from the wall speaker of the room. "This is the Communications Dome. Missile approaching! Missile—"

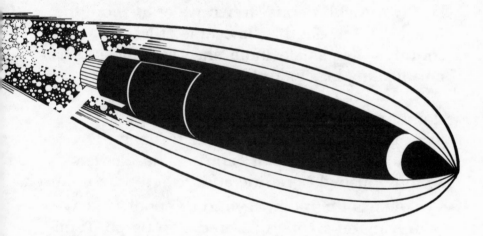

A sound too great to be heard folded all around them. Johnny felt himself picked up and carried away at an angle upward. He ducked away from the ceiling, but the ceiling was no longer there. For a second, still moving, he was in a little box of air, with water all around him. Then the water closed in on him, he felt himself seeming to fly apart in all directions, and he lost track abruptly of what was going on.

. . . At some time later when he came back to
his senses, he and the world about him were moving
very fast. He was rushing through the water in
the black suit of cold-water skins he had never
taken off and his mask was over his face, in
position. Baldur was with him. He had hold of
the dolphin's reins and Baldur was towing him
swiftly through debris-strewn water at about the
fifteen-fathom depth. They came at last to
Johnny's own small-Home, sheared almost in half
and floating loggily in the surrounding water.

The pool entrance was missing. Neta, Sara's
dolphin, was frantically trying the impossible
feat of entering the small-Home through the
air-iris, all unmindful of Tantrums beside her.
Johnny pushed her aside and dove through himself.

Across the room, beyond the pool, he saw
Sara lying on a couch covered by a drape. Tomi
was sitting huddled with his knees together on a
hassock beside the couch. Johnny ran around the
pool and dropped on his knees by the couch.

"My mommy's not feeling good," Tomi said.

Johnny looked at Sara. The world, which had
been moving so fast about him, slowed and
stopped. All things came to an end, and stopped.

Sara lay still, on her back. There was a
little blood dried at the corners of her mouth.
Her eyes were not quite closed. They looked from

under her eyelids at nothing in particular and
her cheeks seemed already sunken in a little
under her high, cold cheekbones.

He stared down at her and a slow and
terrible chill began to creep gradually through
him. He could not take his eyes off her still
face. Slowly he began to shiver. The shivers
increased until he shuddered through his whole
body and his teeth chattered. He saw Tomi coming
toward him with arms outstretched to put them
around his father. And suddenly Johnny broke the
spell holding him and shoved the boy back, away
from him, so hard he staggered.

"Stay away from me!" Johnny shouted. The
room tilted and spun around him. The eye of the
killer whale rushed abruptly like death upon
him through the wall behind the couch, and he
fell forward into roaring nothingness.

When he came back after this, it was to find
Tomi clinging to him and sobbing. Johnny awoke
as somebody might who had been asleep for a long
night. The great gust of feeling that had
whirled him into unconsciousness was gone. He
felt numbed and coldly clear-headed.
Automatically he soothed Tomi. Reflexively he
went about the small-Home, pulling out a sea-sled
and loading it with clothing, medical supplies,

weapons and other equipment for living off the sea.

When it was loaded he took it outside and left Tomi, now also dressed in cold-water skins, fins and mask, to harness Baldur to it. He himself went back inside.

He set straight the drape over Sara and stood a little while looking down at her body. Then he detached the governor from the small-Home's heating element and went back outside. Together, he and Tomi watched as the small-Home caught fire inside.

Collapsing inward, as its walls melted, it sank away from them, a flickering light into dark depths, with Neta and her pup circling bewilderedly down after it.

"Where are we going?" said Tomi, as Johnny handed a rein to Tomi and took one himself.

"Where you'll be safe," said Johnny. He put the boy's other hand on a rail of the sled.

"All by ourselves?" said Tomi.

"Yes." Johnny broke off suddenly. Inside Tomi's mask, he saw the boy pale and frowning, the way Sara had been used to frown. Something moved in Johnny's guts. "All right," he said; but he did not say it to Tomi.

He touched the radio controls of his mask with his tongue, turning the circle of reception up to full. A roar of conversations sounded like surf in his ears.

"This is Johnny Joya," he said into the mike.
"Are there any Council members listening?" The
surf-sound of voices roared on unchanging. "This
is Johnny Joya speaking. Are there any Council
members who can hear me?"

There seemed no change in the sound coming
into his earphone. He turned to Tomi, shrugging.
And then the roar began to diminish a little.
It slackened. "This is Johnny Joya," he said.
"Are there any Council members listening?"

The voices dwindled, faded and disappeared.
Silence roared instead in his earphone. From
far away, blurredly, a single voice spoke.

"Johnny? Johnny, is that you? "This is
Eva Loy. Johnny, we're the only Council members
left. I found the room. None of the rest got
out." She hesitated. "Johnny, can you hear me?
Where are you?"

"North of you," said Johnny. "And swimming
north." There was a cold, clean, dead feeling
in him, like a man might experience after an
amputation when the pain was blocked. "I'm
taking my son, my dolphin and sea-camping
equipment and I'm heading out."

"Heading out?"

"Yes," said Johnny.

He touched the rein and moved it and Baldur
began to swim, pulling the sled and the two

humans with it. Through the rushing gray-blue
water, Johnny saw the young arm and hand of Tomi
in its black sleeve clinging to the sled rail;
and he remembered Patrick's arm, older and
larger, seen in the same position. "The rest of
you should do the same thing."

"Head out?" Eva's voice faded for a second
in the earphone. "Out into the sea
without small-Homes?"

"That's right," said Johnny. He watched
Baldur sliding smoothly through the water.
"Castle-Home is gone. By this time the other
Castle-Homes are probably gone, too. We're
Homeless, now. Everybody might as well face that."

"But we're going to have to build new Homes."

"We can't," said Johnny. "With Patrick
helping, the Landers'll just go on
destroying them."

"But we've got to have Homes!"

"No," said Johnny. A strap on the sled was
working loose. He reached forward automatically
and unbuckled it. "That's what the Landers think.
But they're wrong. Everyone of the third
generation and lots of the second have lived off
the sea without Homes, for the fun of it. We
can do it permanently. We can take care of the
older people, as well, if necessary."

"But," Eva's voice came stronger in the

earphone for a second, "we'll be nothing but a
lot of water-gypsies!"

She fell silent, as if she had suddenly run
out of words.

"No," said Johnny. He pulled the strap
tight and buckled it again. It held well this
time. "Our Homes were something we brought to
the sea from the land. Sooner or later we were
bound to leave them behind and live like true
People of the sea. The Land's just pushed us to
it a little early." He checked the other straps.
They were all tight. "I'm only telling you what
I think—what I'm going to be doing myself. You can
all make your own choices."

There was a long moment of rushing silence
in the earphone. Then Eva's voice called out.

"Johnny! You aren't leaving us?"

"Yes," said Johnny.

"But some day we'll be carrying the fight
back to the Landers. We need you to plan for
then. We need you—"

"No!" The word came out so harshly that
Johnny saw Tomi flinch alongside him and stare
in his direction. "I've helped too much already.
Get someone else to make your plans!"

He felt Tomi's eyes reach into him, and
Sara's ghost hand on his shoulder. He reached
into himself for calmness. For a moment he had

almost come back to life, but now the safe
feeling, the cold, clean, dead feeling, took him
over once again.

"No," he said, more quietly. "You don't
want my help, Eva. And besides, my wife is dead
and I made her a promise to keep our boy safe.
That's all the job I have now. I wouldn't take
any other if I could. If you'll take a last
piece of advice, though, you'll all scatter the
way I'm doing. Spread out through the seas,
we'll be safe."

He turned off his mike, then turned it on.

"Good-by, Eva," he said. "Good-by, People.
Good luck to you all."

Eva's voice spoke again, but Johnny no
longer listened. He picked up the reins and
turned Baldur's head a little to the northeast,
along the water road of the North Atlantic
Current. He shut his mind to all the past.

Baldur responded smoothly. He swam easily
and not too fast, in the graceful underwater up
and down weaving motion of the dolphin that
brought him occasionally to the surface to breathe.
In the earphone, the perplexed conversations
picked up once more.

Johnny did not listen. He felt emptied of
all emotion. Of sorrow, of bitterness, of fear,
of anger. He looked ahead and northward into a

future as wide and empty as the Arctic waters.
Only the wild wastes of the endless oceans were
left now to the people of the sea. They would
gather at Castle-Home no more.

He thought that he had no feeling left
in him; and that this was a good thing.
Then, in his earphones, he heard one of the
parting People begin to sing:

Hey, Johnny! Hey-a, Johnny!
Home from the shore . . .

And other voices took it up, joining in.
The earphone echoed to a spreading chorus.

Hey-o, Johnny! Hey, Johnny!
To high land go no more!

The song blended in many voices. It
reached through the cold, dead feeling of
amputation in him to the awareness that had
come as he stood in the Conference Room and felt
the beating lives of the hundred and twenty-nine
prisoners as if he held them in his hands.

It took hold of him as he had been taken
hold of, in the moment of perception that had
linked him with the other ex-Cadets as, deafened
and smoke-blinded, they made their escape
into the East River. He had cut himself loose
from his people. But he saw now he could not
escape them. No, never could he escape them, any
more than a molecule of water, in its long journey
by sky and mountain and field and harbor-mouth,
could escape its eventual homecoming
to the salt sea. And the knowledge of this,
discovered at last, brought a sort of sad
comfort to him.

He opened his mouth to sing with them;
but—as in the small-Home returning from
Manhattan Island—he found the words would not
come. He held to the sled, listening. About him,
three fathoms of water pressed against his
passage. Baldur swam strongly to the north.
The Atlantic Drift was carrying them east and
north and in time they could come to the
Irminger Current, swinging north between the
Iceland coast and the Greenland shore . . . he, his
son, and his dolphin. They would survive.

Baldur swam strongly, as if he could sense
the purpose of their going. Behind, in his
earphone, Johnny could hear the voices of the
singers beginning to fade and dwindle as they

moved out of range. The number of their voices lessened and became distant.

The sun was going down. The three of them broke surface for a moment and the cloud-heavy sky above was darkening gray. Soon it would be full dark, and somewhere in the black water under the stars they would camp and sleep. Tomi held without a word to the sled. The dolphin swam with strength to the north and east. Behind, the last voices were failing, until only one still sounded, faintly in the earphone:

> *Long away, away, my Johnny!*
> *Four long years and more.*
> *Hey-o, Johnny! Hey, Johnny!*
> *Go to land, no more.*

And still the three of them swam to the north, under a gray sky that was like a road, and forever-flowing.

Editor's note: 207
Ms. Miesel, noted sf critic,
is considered by the author
to be the foremost critical
authority on his work.

An Afterword

by Sandra Miesel

"Land and Sea have got to get together—or destroy each other. They're . . . the same people! Maybe with different shells of flesh and blood, but with the same human spirit in them, fighting, crying to break free!"

—*The Space Swimmers,*
by Gordon R. Dickson

Just as the Land and Sea must come together in order to free the common spirit they share, so must *Home from the Shore* be read along with its sequel *The Space Swimmers* to fully grasp the message contained in both stories. *Home from the Shore* sets up the problem—the hostile divorce between Land and Sea—which is solved through a welcome reconciliation in *The Space Swimmers*. Taken together, the novels show humanity facing crises of survival and growth. Mankind finally begins to acquire the power of controlling its own evolution and must decide how to use this power wisely. Balanced growth proves to be the only route to species survival.

Land and Sea represent that familiar pair of Dicksonian opposites, the unconscious/ conservative and conscious/ progressive sides of human nature. Unless the warring factions of the race achieve a bond of unity, they will perish. Unless the conflicting tendencies within a person form a single Self, he cannot be sane. Dickson expresses his theme of polarities uniting by setting pairs of groups, characters, phenomena, ideas, and images in parallel and recording their interactions. Duality becoming identity provides both the message and the medium for these two novels.

First, there is the fundamental distinction between the peoples of the Land and the Sea. The Land owns man's past. It is heir to the accomplishments of all previous generations but at present has largely given up trying to accomplish anything further itself. Unable to colonize the stars, the frustrated Landers put all their energies into a futile status-scramble called the Game of Life. They find little satisfaction in ordinary work or play or even in personal relationships. Their society is highly class-conscious. The quasi-feudal Groups (occupational organizations) offer their members security in exchange for wearing a Mark (badge).

On the other hand, man's future belongs to the Sea. In only four generations, the Sea-dwellers have grown larger, stronger, quicker than the Landers. Rapid evolutionary changes have sharpened their senses and awakened new kinds of perceptions in them. "It was not here as it was on the land, where men relied on mechanical devices and social order, but by their own strengths and skills his People were lords of the sea." The Sea People are as proud of their freedom as of their talents. Their egalitarian, vibrantly personal society is held together by strong communal loyalties.

But the Land envies the Sea its gifts and fears eventual domination by it despite a thousand-fold advantage in population and incalculable superiority in wealth and technology. The Sea People are too busy being elite to reassure them properly. The opening chapters of *Home from the Shore* show the prejudices of both sides in action.

Finally, the Landers try to deny the Sea People's humanity and hunt them down like animals. The pogrom is aptly symbolized by a leopard seal's pursuit of a tame dolphin in the first pages of The Space Swimmers. The seal tries to kill its irritating quarry so it can be left alone to eat, sleep, and "forget strange things." But the mentally and physically superior dolphin refrains from killing the other because it has obligations to fulfill elsewhere.

Land and Sea face a tragic dilemma: each side has the means to exterminate the other yet each has fatal deficencies only the other can supply. The stagnant Land must expand off-planet; the progressive Sea needs a stabilizing cultural matrix. This is why the closing of the Space Academy and the scattering of the Sea People are such traumas, aside from the accompanying loss of life. Only when Land and Sea pull back from Armageddon and recognize their common human identity can all mankind share the best qualities of both sides. Then humans will be able to reach the stars—and even beyond.

The traits of each bloc are embodied in human and non-human characters. Two huge animals stand for the most ominous tendencies of Land and Sea. In *The Space Swimmers*, Mugger, an immensely old giant squid who is weak with hunger and obsessed with nothing but food, represents the Land while an unnamed killer whale represents the Sea in *Home from the Shore*. The latter is the more dangerous of the two because of its high intelligence. The fearless, pitiless killer whale follows an ethic in which there is "neither wife nor child, nor friend nor enemy—but only truth and what the mind desired." One beast clings to marginal survival without progress; the other pursues a selfish, rootless freedom. Due to the structure of their heads, only one eye of each creature is shown at a time in symbolic warning of their incompleteness.

But young Tomi Joya can communicate with both monsters. He turns the squid's thoughts to something else besides food for a moment and makes a killer whale his personal "sea-friend." These unprecedented feats spring from Tomi's gift for total identification with all other living things. Remember, Tomi is short for Thomas which means "Twin."

This gift equips Tomi to make contact with the Space Swimmers. These intelligent, space-dwelling aliens are virtually immortal, spectacularly free, and unshakably responsible—noble role models for evolving man. The Swimmers themselves resolve the issue their presence raises. Man must develop to an equivalent ethical level in order to copy their method of travel between the stars. The requirements of fictional plot and philosophical principle unite here.

Since Tomi's communications breakthrough answers the questions asked by *Home from the Shore* and *The Space Swimmers*, he is the novels' true hero. As the first born—and best born—of the Sea People's fourth generation, he is the most highly evolved member of the human race. This son of "Joy" and "Light" is a sign of hope for the future. He is "the bud and the shoot and the bloom of eternity itself."

On the other hand, Tomi's father and precursor Johnny Joya is the novels' protagonist. Although wonderfully endowed in mind and body, he is not as perfect as Tomi. He has a streak of killer whale recklessness within him to overcome by learning responsibility for others. Johnny accomplishes this by meeting himself in Tomi and by inheriting the protectiveness of his wife Sarah Light after her death. In every sense, Johnny makes Tomi and hence Tomi's victory possible. He creates situations in which Tomi can exist and triumph.

As the pivotal character in the two novels, Johnny pairs in turn with each of the other major characters, the four fuses capable of detonating the world like a bomb. He and his cousin Pat grow up with the closeness of twin brothers, become estranged in *Home from the Shore,* and reforge their bond of unity in *The Space Swimmers.* Johnny and Matig Marieanna recognize an inner identity that instantly makes them lovers in *The Space Swimmers.* This compensates for the lack of mutual understanding between Johnny and Sarah in *Home from the Shore.* (Apparently, love at first sight is lasting among the Sea People because of their keen intuition.) Pat avoids looking too closely at Matig lest he feel the same attraction Johnny does and spoil his match with his own beloved Mila Jhan.

These pairings result in happy unions but Johnny can find no common ground with Construction Baron Barth Stuve and Transportation Baron Kai Ebberly. Therefore he must destroy them. Johnny's seasoned personality with its rough-hewn harmony of progressive and conservative qualities makes him the uncompromising enemy of both men. Stuve, whose Mark is the compass and plumb bob, champions the evolutionary status quo. Ebberly, whose Mark is two interlocked wheels, is an irresponsible megalomaniac. Each is as incomplete as the squid and the whale. Each offers a fatally false blueprint for man's future.

The phenomenon of magnetism and the principle of balance undergird the novels as prime expressions of Dickson's duality into unity theme. A magnet is a single entity with two oppositely signed, mutually attractive poles. A balance exists at one point between two offsetting forces. The author plays clever variations on these concepts, interpreting them in every sense, from the proverbial to the scientific to the philosophical. He builds them directly into the plot. For example, balance gives Johnny victory over Stuve, magnetism over Ebberly.

Magnetism as a physical phenomenon is a key feature of Sea technology: boats and people alike are enclosed in protective magnetic envelopes. (The same treatment is later extended to spaceships and spacesuits.) At the physiological level, sensitivity to magnetic flux is the basis of the Sea People's uncanny powers of orientation and location. These powers also make them ideal spacemen, both in the conventional manner planned by the Landers and in the unconventional one discovered by the Joyas. Because sea and space are comparable environments, mastery of one leads to mastery of the other.

Easy familiarity with the properties of magnetism in devices and talents links the Sea People to the Swimmers. The space creatures are essentially sentient gas clouds enclosed in natural magnetic envelopes. They glide across the galactic seas on cur-

rents of magnetic force just as Sea Homes follow
ocean currents. Evolution is pointing the Sea People
in the same direction as the majestic, mature Swimmers—forward. Both groups are hated, then feared
by the Land because they possess marvelous powers
the Landers cannot share. " 'We were like the space
bats to them,' " says Johnny, describing the Landers'
attitude.

The Sea People's instinctive feelings of kinship
and sympathy toward the Swimmers trigger their
rejection of the Land in *Home from the Shore*. Because they protested the netting and death of the
Swimmers, they, too, are liable to be captured and
killed. Neither Swimmers nor Sea folk will submit
and yield up their secrets to the Land. The Joyas'
success convincing the Swimmers that they and the
Sea People "be of one blood" parallels their efforts
to convince the Land of the same thing and brings
The Space Swimmers to its happy conclusion.

The Swimmers' method of space travel depends
upon magnetism and balance. They move along the
web of magnetic forces by introducing temporary
imbalances into the system and allowing the correc-
tion to propel them onward. (This also illustrates the
evolutionary principle that progress is made in re-
sponse to stress.) To seaborn senses, the web looks
like a system of roads or girders—but neither Transportation nor Construction Baron will ever rule
them.

Not only does the web maintain its internal
equilibrium, it balances the properties of the physical universe which it pervades and surrounds. The
relationship symbolizes the harmony between the
immaterial and material aspects of existence. Each

microcosmic balance repeats the macrocosmic one. Every atom in a lodestone, every cell in an organism, every individual in a society pursues its own kind of balance.

Johnny's initial problems with personal relationships exemplify this issue. He must struggle to attain the spiritual equanimity that comes naturally to Tomi. In *Home from the Shore,* Johnny and Sarah are incompatible extremes—he too rash, she too cautious. But the shock of her death restructures his life because it forces new responsibilities upon him. Being a father is a greater challenge than being Cadet Representative at the Space Academy. Only after stabilizing his own personality during a self-imposed exile can Johnny come home to his People in *The Space Swimmers.* Only then can he become the wise leader he was born to be.

The patterns of separation and reunion experienced by Johnny, Pat, and their People illustrate the necessity of balance in social dynamics. Other types of balance can be treated as arrays of linear forces—picture a scale or see-saw. But the interaction between centripetal and centrifugal forces provides a better model for the relationship between the whole and its parts. Too much centripetal force will draw an orbiting component toward the center of the system; too much centrifugal force will drive it off at a tangent. Pat resists domination by Lander values while living among them. Johnny alters his independent course. Both return to play useful roles within their community. Likewise, the Sea must be neither slave nor master of the Land; neither absorbed by it nor aloof from it. The two sides must form a stable partnership.

Humanity can only survive if its members strike a healthy balance among themselves. The group and the individual need one another. A responsible group permits individual freedom; a free individual shows responsibility towards his group. This is why the Sea's divorce from the Land and Johnny's exile from his People are futile as well as dangerous steps. Johnny realizes this even as he flees. "He had cut himself loose from his People. But he saw now he could not escape them. No, never could he escape them, any more than a molecule of water, in its long journey by sky and mountain and field and harbor-mouth, could escape its eventual homecoming to the salt sea."

Furthermore, the leader and the followers within any group also need one another. They imply and define each other. As Matig explains: "The same instincts that make us follow Johnny as our natural leader make it impossible for him to refuse to lead us—if he knows the People really need and want him as a whole." This mutual psychological magnetism resembles the social order in migratory birds, creatures whose instincts are believed to operate under the influence of the earth's magnetic field. Thus, mentions of geese flying south in autumn and swans flying north in spring which open and close *The Space Swimmers* tie the concepts of balance and magnetism together on several levels. They recall the gladness with which the People follow Johnny from shore to sea and from sea to shore. By ending with a glimpse of the nobler and rarer species, Dickson expresses his confidence that one day the age-old condition of mankind will be transformed so that: "More swans than geese will live/ Less fools than wise."

The two flocks of birds migrating in opposite directions are one example of many paired images the author uses to establish an atmosphere of duality. Season and time provide thematic cues in both novels. The original version of *Home from the Shore* begins in midafternoon on a bright midsummer day and ends near dusk on a gloomy day about one week later. *The Space Swimmers* opens with simultaneous midafternoon scenes on a bright spring day in Antarctica and a gloomy autumn one in Georgia. It closes on a clear morning near dawn six months later. Note that only the land feels changes in time and season. The sea, like space, knows none: Yet descriptions of these events, like the accompanying movements of characters between northern and southern hemispheres of the globe, help impart a stately tidal rhythmn to the stories.

The same pattern of duality appears in details like Stuve's deformed, furclad shoulders opposed to Johnny's bare, perfect ones as well as in plot structures. *Home from the Shore* is essentially the story of Johnny's flight to his People and then away from them. The seal-dolphin chase ending in death that begins *The Space Swimmers* is matched by Johnny's friendship-forging pursuit of a Swimmer near the conclusion.

Persistent motifs like eyes, gates, boundaries, passages—interfaces of all kinds—indicate transitions from one state to another but visions of the opposing states united are mostly confined to characters' imaginations. The land-based and sea-going laboratories that couple and go into space in order to successfully complete their research is one exception. An even more intriguing one is the sym-

bolic trinity of primary colors that repeats throughout the novels: red light on land for the body, blue
light under the sea for the mind, and golden light on
the star roads for the spirit. No color is specified for
the "unquenchable illumination" shining over *The
Space Swimmer's* finale but it might be pictured as
the red and gold rays of sunrise spread against the
bright blue sky.

Both in theme and treatment, *Home from the
Shore* and *The Space Swimmers* resemble Dickson's
most famous work, the Childe Cycle. When completed, the Cycle will consist of three historical,
three contemporary, and six science fiction novels.
Dorsai! (1959), *Necromancer* (1962), "Warrior"
(1965), *Soldier, Ask Not* (1968), *Tactics of Mistake*
(1971), and "Brothers" (1973) have appeared so far.
The concluding sf novels, *The Final Encyclopedia*
and *Childe* are currently in preparation. The Cycle's
subject is the maturation of the human race. It traces
the course of human evolution from the fourteenth
to the twenty-fourth centuries showing how the
conscious/ progressive and unconscious/ conservative aspects of our collective racial psyche are finally
integrated into one fully-evolved, balanced Self.

The similarity of theme between the Cycle and
the pair of novels under discussion here is partly due
to timing—the short version of *Home from the Shore*
was published in 1962, the original edition of *The
Space Swimmers* in 1967. But the most important
reason for the resemblance is the author's intense
commitment to the ideas themselves. Man's destiny,
says Dickson, is to be free, responsible, and creative. Like all intelligent beings, man is constantly
evolving towards perfection. The crucial step in

every life form's progress, the one that completes its initiation, is achieving conscious control over its own evolution. Only then can maturity begin.

Dickson always dramatizes growth as a sequence of events—separation, independent development, and reunion. In the Childe Cycle, the process occurs on an interstellar scale. Splinter Cultures develop unique talents on different planets but the whole human race will ultimately benefit from their experiments. *Home from the Shore* and *The Space Swimmers* are only concerned with terrestrial events and a single separatist group but the pattern is similar. The history of intelligent life on earth is a pilgrimage back and forth between sea and land before culminating in space. Johnny with his repeated exiles and homecomings epitomizes the process; Tomi exemplifies its fulfillment. Together they convince both Land and Sea of the evolutionary ethic which Johnny summarizes as "the concepts of *freedom, responsibility,* and *work*—and particularly *work.*" These are the same values which will prevail with the emergence of full-spectrum Responsible Man at the Cycle's close.

Comparing personalitites, Johnny most resembles Cletus Graham in *Tactics of Mistake*. Both are forerunners and prototypes of the hero to come (Tomi and the three incarnations of *Dorsai!*'s Donal Graeme). They divide squabbling factions of humanity which their heirs will reunite. Ebberly is like de Castries, the foe of Cletus, and Donal's enemy William is like Stuve.

But despite all these points in common, *Home from the Shore* and *The Space Swimmers* echo only the duality theme of the Cycle. These novels do not emphasize Dickson's growth-spurring triad of Prime Characters—the Men of Faith, Philosophy, and War—or any of their attendant symbols. Concepts and characters are grouped by twos rather than by threes in *Home from the Shore* and *The Space Swimmers*.

Here the protagonist and the hero combine with a pair of allies against a pair of adversaries and they all dance intricate measures together. Pat mirrors Johnny; Tomi duplicates him; Matig does something of both. Johnny and Pat stand for the better qualities of progress and conservatism while Ebberly and Stuve stand for the worse. Matig's doomsday threat offsets Ebberly's; Pat's design for reunion contradicts Stuve's. Pat directly aids Johnny against Stuve as Tomi does against Ebberly. In every instance, counterparts who can unite, prevail.

Finally, the same system of comparative mythology that unlocks the meaning of the Cycle may be usefully applied to *Home from the Shore* and *The Space Swimmers*. A proper interpretation of the Cycle is possible only in the light of recent work by controversial European mythologist Georges Dumézil and it is important for understanding the other two novels as well.

Dumézil maintains that all Indo-European-speaking peoples characteristically divide their gods, heroes, and social orders into three basic categories which he calls "functions." These functions are sovereignty, force, and nourishment. The first function splits into two halves specializing in magical (magicians, priests, poets—rule of inspiration) and legal (sages, kings as lawgivers—rule of reason) sovereignty. The second function includes all expressions of physical strength (warriors and kings as leaders). The third function covers fertility, peace, and well-being (food producers and artisans). Slaves, barbarians, outcasts, and popular entertainers occupied a fourth category outside the system.

Although Dickson wrote his stories without any knowledge whatsoever of Dumézil's theories, interesting relationships appear when the cast of *Home from the Shore* and *The Space Swimmers* are placed in their functional slots.

functions	characters	Cycle Prime Characters	
1 (magic) 1 (law)	Pat the Bard Johnny as Thinker	Man of Faith Man of Philosophy	Tomi
2 (force)	Johnny as Leader	Man of War	Tomi
3 (nourishment)	Matig the Scientist		
4 (outsiders)	Mila the Entertainer		

Potentially at least, Tomi combines all functional qualities like an ideal king. The pair of adult couples cover the full range of human activities at work and at play. They can organize, defend, maintain, and amuse their community. Intuitive, artistic talents match rational, scientific ones. Abstract and concrete gifts meet. The inmost and outmost, highest and lowest levels join.

Such completeness is not always found in Dickson's fiction. The movers and shakers in the Childe Cycle occupy only the first two levels while their opponents usually cluster in the third. However, all functions are represented favorably in *Time Storm* (1977), an independent novel which expresses views on evolution and unification similar to those in *Home from the Shore* and *The Space Swimmers*. *Time Storm*'s hero is as persistent as Johnny and as capable of identifying with other beings as Tomi.

Thus, from scientific foundation to mystical summit, Dickson builds his stories with an efficiency that is almost relentless. The message emerges naturally and inevitably from the medium, a literary approach the author calls "consciously thematic." Every component—great or small—is raw material for the author's purpose: the names, faces, personalities, garb of human and animal characters; time, place, season, weather, and scenery; technology and social customs; even verses of songs and allusions to Kipling. No detail is merely gratuitous. Each element fits into Dickson's grand design, a vision of the murky, destructive conflicts within man yielding to creative, light-drenched harmony.